BEAUTIFUL ILLUSIONS DUET BOOK TWO

BEAUTIFUL
Ever After

GEORGIA CATES

Imprint: Georgia Cates Books, LLC

ISBN-13: 978-1-948113-14-4

ISBN-10: 1-948113-14-7

Editing services provided by Lisa Aurello

Formatting by Jeff Senter of Indie Formatting Services

Cover design by Georgia Cates

MAXWELL HUTCHESON

Lou. She came into my life and became my world. My everything. It's that simple.

Brady opens the door and shakes his head when he looks at me. "You dumb bastard. You were supposed to fuck her and let her go when the arrangement ended."

"Aye, that was the plan." But plans change. And mine certainly did.

He steps out of the doorway, making room for me to enter. "Get the hell in here, and let's sort out this fucking mess you've gotten yourself into."

"Aye, but whisky first."

Brady pours two Tomatins and I toss mine back before he picks up his glass. "Hit me again, mate."

He pours another whisky three fingers high, and I throw it back, same as the first.

"Another?"

"No." I can't be steamin' while we try to figure out what the hell I'm going to do.

I place the whisky glass on the table and run my

palms down my face, groaning. "Everything was fine this morning. We were fine."

We. Were. Fine.

"Maybe *you* were fine but she wasn't? Did anything seem off?"

"She was crying this morning when I woke up."

Brady chuckles. "When a woman cries, it's usually a strong indication that she definitely isn't fine."

"It sounds bad when I say it aloud, I know, but we talked and everything seemed to be all right. She stopped crying and we had sex... and everything seemed okay. Before I left for work, I told her to choose something special for tonight, and she told me that she would. She was okay."

"Why were you doing something special tonight?"

"Our Inamorata arrangement was ending at midnight."

"Ahh... I hate to break it to you, you brilliant motherfucker, but I think your inamorata left because she didn't want to go through saying goodbye."

"But I wasn't going to say goodbye. I was planning to ask Lou for a real relationship. No contract or any of that other Inamorata shite."

"I figured as much. I've seen that one coming for a while."

"I don't think avoiding a goodbye was Lou's reason for leaving early. Mrs. McVey told me Blair came to the house. She said Lou was in tears afterward."

"So you find Lou and straighten out this mess. Ask her to be your girlfriend or whatever it is you want out of a relationship with her. Problem solved."

If only it were that easy. "Finding her is going to be difficult when I don't know her last name or where she lives."

"Cora knows."

"Already been to see her. She won't tell me anything."

"That's not surprising. The survival of her business is dependent upon discretion and privacy. Without those things, she has nothing."

"I understand Cora's position and I'm not angry at her." She called Lou on my behalf. I can't ask more of her than that.

"Let's go over what you know to be fact. What do you know about Lou's life outside of Inamorata?"

"Her real name is Cait. I'm sure it's a shortened version of Caitriona. Or maybe Catherine?"

"All common names so that's not helpful."

Her father and his family live in Edinburgh, but I don't remember ever hearing her call them by their names. Also not helpful.

"Her best friend's name is Rachel."

"I met Lou's best friend at the cocktail party, and she introduced her as Meg."

"Meg would be her Inamorata name. Her real name is Rachel. I confirmed that when I went to the building where they used to live. A tenant remembered a pair of roommates named Cait and Rachel who recently moved out."

Brady's eyes narrow the way they always do when he's in deep thought. "Their former landlord might be able to tell you their last names. Or a forwarding address. Unless, of course, he's upstanding and respects their privacy enough to withhold that information."

"He could probably be bought."

"And if he can't?" Brady asks.

"She was planning to return to the University of Edinburgh. Maybe I could use that as a way to find her?"

"Without a last name, that's no help. You're reduced to walking around campus, hoping you'll see her."

Ian will be there. I could ask him to be on the lookout for her, but he'd ask why she left me and why I have no idea how to reach her. I don't want him to know the details of our relationship.

Those details are our secret.

"She has an ex-boyfriend. His name is Cameron Stewart. He's a bartender and works in Edinburgh. Or at least he did."

"Finally. A first and last name. That's helpful information."

"It's helpful until you factor in that he's trying to win Lou back." He isn't likely to help me just as I wouldn't help him when he wanted me to tell Lou to call him.

"The guy is a bartender. His knowledge about her could easily be bought."

It would kill me to have to go to that fucker. "I'll only consider it after all other options have been exhausted."

"Then let's go back to Lou's best friend. I met her at the cocktail party. She was with a client. A regular, Lou said." Brady's brow wrinkles. "His name was Clyde or Claud. Something like that and he owns tour companies, the ones with all-day excursions around Scotland."

"Well that's slightly better than looking for a needle in a haystack."

"You can get to Rachel through this Clyde or Claud and ask her to put you in contact with Lou. If she won't, Cameron Stewart can be your next move. After that, you may be forced to hire a private investigator."

I'd prefer to not take that route. Thomas is dirty. Very dirty. And I don't know which private investigators are and aren't on his payroll.

"Lou told me she loved me." After we made love, skin on skin, an act that she believes should only be shared by two people in love. That alone tells me how she feels about me. The words weren't necessary, but I coveted hearing them from her.

Her 'I love you' doesn't accompany motive. It comes from a place of honesty. Her heart.

"Did you say it back?"

"No."

I wasn't expecting her to say those words to me. I wasn't prepared. And when I didn't say them back, I hated the hurt that I saw in her eyes.

I was afraid to love her. Now, I'm more afraid to lose her.

I'm such a fucking dobber. I should have told her right then and there how I felt about her.

"Do you love the lass?"

"I do." I love her so much it hurts. "And I should have told her so, but I was afraid."

"Don't beat yourself up over it. Mina put you through some intense shite. No one can blame you for being cautious."

I foolishly let her get away without telling her

how I feel. "Caution may have caused me to lose the only thing that's ever made me feel alive."

"If she's the one, you'll find her and tell her. Simple as that."

The one. Is that even possible? I've only known Lou for three months.

"I made myself believe that Mina was the one and look at how wrong I was about that. How can I trust myself to get it right this time?"

"I don't think I'm the person to ask. In case you forgot, I got it wrong too. But if I had to guess at what kind of advice to give you, I'd say listen to your gut this time and not Thomas Lochridge."

Brady has that much right.

I wasn't ready to get married but Thomas Lochridge was clear about my options. No marriage meant no promotion. The only way I was going to climb the ladder at the firm was as his son-in-law. Because Mina was ready to be a wife. And what Mina wanted, Mina got. Thomas always saw to that.

Somewhere along the way, I was sucked into all there was to gain, but the cost was so much more than I could have ever imagined.

I thought things were complicated before Lou, but my problems multiplied tenfold when she entered my life. Having her is going to cost me. I know that. There's never been any doubt in my mind about it. I'll probably lose everything. And I don't care. Having everything means nothing without her.

She is worth the fall.

2

CAITRIONA LOUDEN

LIGHT BLUE FOCUSED ON HAZEL. HARD, CHISELED ARMS holding me. Warm flesh on flesh, two bodies fused as one.

That's how I choose to remember us.

Sweet dreams. There have been none of those for me. A nearly sleepless night has forced me to think about the beautiful ever after I'm never going to have with the man I love so dearly.

Fate, you've been a cruel bastard to me once again. Why am I your favorite person to hurt?

A soft knock on the door accompanies my whispered name. "Are you awake?"

"I am. You can come in."

Rachel opens the door and enters the room, sitting on the side of the bed. "Did you sleep at all?"

"Not much."

"I was afraid of that. Do you want to stay in today and rest instead of going shopping?"

"I'm tired but I need so many things. I don't even

have a toothbrush." Or tampons. And I'll be needing those soon.

"You don't have to go today. You can borrow anything you need from me and we can go tomorrow after you've had some rest."

I doubt I'll sleep tonight either. "There's no need in putting it off."

"A hot shower and a good breakfast. That'll make you feel better."

That's doubtful. I don't think anything is going to make me feel better. And I'm afraid that nothing ever will.

"I'll need to borrow something to wear."

"You're always welcome to anything that belongs to me."

"I know. And thank you."

This is a rare moment—Rachel taking care of me. I'm usually the one who mothers her. But she doesn't need me anymore. She has Claud to take care of her.

And I have no one.

Claud's driver stops the car in front of our favorite department store. "Would you like me to wait for you or should I return later?"

"We have a lot of shopping to do so we'll probably be a while. I'll text you when we're ready to be picked up."

"Aye, Miss Rachel," the driver says.

She smiles when I do a double take after the driver calls her by her real name. "I'll explain in a minute."

We get out of the car and Rachel says, "I left

Inamorata to be Claud's girlfriend. His real girl-friend. It would be silly to have him and the staff call me Meg, don't you think?"

"Yeah. Of course." Makes total sense.

Rachel and Claud are real. Hutch and I were not. At least not on his end. What I felt was real.

I'm happy for Rachel—very happy—but I admit that I envy her relationship. "Claud's good for you."

"I know, right? He's exactly what I needed in my life."

Truth. I love Rachel but she needs someone to take care of her. That's who she is and I don't see that changing anytime soon. She's lucky Claud wants to be her keeper.

"What would you like to look at first?"

"Bras and panties." I went commando today because I refuse to borrow Rachel's. She may be my best friend but I just can't wear her underwear.

She holds up a cute little black lace G-string. "Nice."

"Nice for you but I have no one to wear that for now. I'm just looking for normal everyday undies." Because no one besides me is going to be seeing them.

"That's boring."

Boring is what I need. "Classes start in two weeks so my life is about to become very busy. I'm jumping headfirst into my studies. It'll be a good distraction."

Rachel sighs and returns the G-string to its place on the table. "Classes and studying aren't going to stop you from thinking about him."

Pity. I've seen it my entire life. And I hate it.

"Yes, I'm sad about leaving Hutch, but I'll eventually get over it. It's not the end of the world." Even if right now it feels like it is.

"You're not a delicate piece of glass that can be easily broken. I know that, but you're wounded and it hurts me to see you like this. I don't like it."

"Trust me. I don't like it either, but it'll get better in time. It won't always hurt like this." The words sound really good coming out of my mouth. I only hope that they'll be true one day.

"Have you thought about going back to Inamorata?"

"What kind of crazy question is that?"

I have an insane amount of money. With frugal spending, I could live on it for years. And after graduation, it will afford me the ability to work on my manuscript without worries about finances. I won't be forced to put away my writing and work at a nine-to-five job to make ends meet.

I have a chance at achieving my dreams, all because of Hutch. I'll never forget that he's the one who made that possible.

"I'm not asking about Inamorata because of the money." She shrugs. "I don't know. Things went so well with Hutch that maybe you'd meet someone else and have an even better experience?"

"I don't want to meet someone else." Ever. Hutch has ruined all other men for me.

"Maybe not today but you will one day." Rachel holds up a pair of granny panties. "And do you really want to be wearing knickers like these when you do?"

"Whether I meet someone or not, I don't ever want to wear panties like those."

"Pretty bras and knickers make a girl feel good

even if she's the only person seeing them. Buy your-self some pretty things. You owe that to yourself."

God knows that I need something to make me feel better. If pretty panties will do it, I'll give it a shot.

Pretty bras and panties. New jeans and tops. Yoga pants and T-shirts. Accessories. None of it makes me feel better. Not even a little. Maybe that's why I didn't buy much. But then again, there's no need to buy a lot of things until I find somewhere to live.

Somewhere to live. That has to be my next focus. I only have two weeks to find a place and get settled before classes begin. It can be done but it's going to be hectic. There's not a minute to waste.

I accepted Rachel's invitation to have dinner with her and Claud. It was nice to not spend the evening alone. But it's bedtime now and that's what I am. Alone.

I wish Rachel would come and invade my bed as she did so many times at the apartment so we could talk. But I know she won't. Claud is going out of town tomorrow. He'll be gone for a week, and he'll want Rachel in his bed tonight.

Just like Hutch wanted me in his bed.

I don't know how much time passes after I throw myself across the bed. It could be seconds, minutes, hours. Elements of time are indistinguishable in this dark place without Hutch.

It's our second night apart. I wonder if he's missing me as he lies beside the empty spot where I used to sleep. Did he wake and reach for me this morning before he remembered that I was gone?

At some point, I become a pathetic, crying wreck. Didn't I swear that this would never be me? That I would never be this woman, the one who lies in the dark crying for a man she can't have?

I'm such a fool.

To regret meeting Hutch would be to wish him away, and I can never do that. Even the briefest time we had together was worth the agony I feel in my heart now.

Maybe tomorrow will be better.

But probably not.

3

MAXWELL HUTCHESON

I wake and reach for Lou, finding the spot on the bed next to me empty. And my heart sinks. Again.

Eight days without her. I thought that I would have found her by now.

It's odd, but I find comfort in spending time with Ava Rose. Being with her reminds me of the days we spent with Lou, days when we felt like a real family.

Calvin is driving us to my parents' house in Glasgow. Ava Rose and I are in the back seat of the car, and she's looking at me. I can't help but wonder if she misses Lou as much as I do. Is she wondering why she's gone? For some reason, I believe she is. "You don't have to worry, lassie. I'm going to bring Lou back to you. Back to both of us."

Ava Rose fusses a wee bit and I stroke my thumb down the center of her forehead and bridge of her nose, a little trick that Lou taught me. It takes a few minutes but the massage eventually soothes her to sleep, same as when Lou used to do it to her.

Lou was always so good with Ava Rose. Just like a real mum would be.

We arrive at my parents' and Mum takes Ava Rose from me. "Lou's not with you?"

"No."

"That's too bad. I was hoping she would be."

I was hoping to put off the Lou conversation until later. I'm not looking forward to discussing it, but I might as well get it over with.

Mum carries Ava Rose into the living room and works on unbuckling her.

"I have something to tell you about Lou."

She lifts Ava Rose out of the car seat and holds her up in the air, making funny faces at her. "Oh, wee lassie. What has your dad done now?"

"Why do you assume that I did something wrong?"

There it is, that I'm-your-mum-and-I-know-everything look. "Is my assumption inaccurate?"

"I've messed up... but it isn't entirely my fault."

"Then which part is your fault?"

I don't look forward to telling my mum half-truths. But I also don't want her to think poorly of Lou or me. That's why I can't confess that Lou was an escort whom I paid a lot of money to be my secret lover. "I guess I should start by admitting that we were seeing each other in secret. The immediate family knew about her but I never had intentions of telling anyone else about our relationship."

"How long have you been sneaking around with her?"

"Three months."

"Trust me. She isn't fine with being your secret,

and if you understood anything about women, you'd already know that."

"Secrecy isn't our problem. I think Blair did something to make Lou leave me."

"Lou is gone?" I hear the disappointment in my mum's voice and it cuts me to the bone.

"She left eight days ago after a visit from Blair. Mrs. McVey told me that Lou was upset and crying after their conversation. I know she did something to her."

"It certainly sounds as though something happened. Have you spoken to Blair?"

"She claims nothing happened between them, but I don't believe that for a second."

"I don't either," Mum says.

"I've reached out to Lou a hundred times, but she won't respond to my texts or take my calls." She's blocked me. I know she has.

"Was everything all right between the two of you before Blair came around?"

"Yes… and no."

"What does yes and no mean?"

I never confided in Mum about my relationship with Mina. It feels a wee bit odd to be discussing my love life with her. "Lou told me she loved me."

Mum's head jolts around and her eyes widen. "She did, huh? What was your response to that?"

She looks so hopeful. And I'm about to shatter it all to pieces.

"I didn't say it back." Instead, I fucked her and told her to close her eyes and she'd be able to feel how important she was to me. What a stupid dobber thing to say to a woman.

I love you. Why didn't I say those words back to her? It would have changed everything. She wouldn't have left me no matter what Blair said. I'm sure of it.

"I think I owe you an apology. It seems I've meddled in your life when I shouldn't have."

"What do you mean?"

"I visited Lou a few weeks ago. She told me she loved you, and I urged her to tell you so because I thought you felt the same. I'm sorry, son. I wouldn't have encouraged her if I had known you didn't have those kinds of feelings for her."

"But I do, Mum. I love Lou very much." I didn't know I could feel this way. I never had these kinds of feelings for Mina.

"But you didn't tell Lou you loved her."

"I hadn't yet worked it out in my head that I loved her too. By the time I realized the truth, she was already gone. She left without knowing that I love her." And that kills me.

"Oh, Max." Mum shakes her head and closes her eyes for at least three beats of my heart. "You were in love with Lou when you brought her home. I knew it the minute I saw the two of you together. And she was so obviously in love with you. She might not have told you yet, but it was so apparent to me."

"I chose to not see it because I didn't want to fall in love with her. But I see the truth now. And I'm going to find her and tell her how I feel. I'm going to make this right."

"It's been over a week. What's taking so long?"

Good question. It's going to be hard to explain why I don't know where Lou lives so I'm choosing to not go there. "She's been very good at evading me."

"Blair must have said or done something terrible to make Lou cut you off like this."

"I'm sure she did but she'll never admit to it."

"That poor lass must be hurting. She believes her love for you is not returned, which would be devastating. It's no wonder she slipped away without a goodbye."

"I've been an asshat. I know that, Mum, but I'm going to make this right with her." I have to. Because the alternative is unacceptable.

"You've hurt Lou in a terrible way. She may not be interested in your making this right. It might be wise to prepare yourself for rejection."

The thought of Lou rejecting me is painful, but it's a reality that I can't ignore. "I'm going to do everything within my power to make it up to her. I hate what my life looks like without her in it. And when I find her, I'm never letting her go again."

"What does never letting her go again mean?"

I hear the question that Mum's not asking.

"Ava Rose and Lou love each other. Lou and I love each other. I'd be a fool to let her get away again." The words are frightening to say out loud, but I need to say them. I need to hear them from my own lips. "I want Lou to be my wife."

Mum's lips part but nothing comes out.

"I know what you're thinking and it's true. We've only known each other for three months, but it's been the happiest three months of my life. She makes me feel alive, more so than I have in years, and I'm miserable without her."

"I think it's wonderful, Max."

"Do you really?"

"I do. But the Lochridges aren't going to think it's

wonderful. You should be prepared for trouble out of them."

"I expect problems, but this is my life and I want Lou in it. They're going to have to accept her."

And fuck them if they don't.

That's what I have to say about that.

4

CAITRIONA LOUDEN

Standing in front of the bathroom mirror, I look at myself. And I grasp the reality of the situation for what it is. I look like hell.

Rachel will be here soon. I don't want her to see me looking as though I'm knocking on death's door so I dab concealer on the dark circles below my lower lids. The cover-up helps to camouflage my lack of sleep, but no amount of makeup is going to hide the sadness in my eyes or my sunken cheeks.

I don't have to get on the scale to confirm that I've lost weight. The clothes I bought two weeks ago are falling off of me. And I don't see that improving anytime soon. I can't eat because my gut is in knots all of the time.

Rachel has brought my favorite foods by every night this week. I've forced down a few bites each time to make her happy, but anything more sends me dashing toward the bathroom. And tonight is no different.

"Three bites of a sandwich aren't enough. You need to eat more."

I love that Rachel is here looking after me. And I want to eat for her. But I can't.

"Believe me, I would if I could but it makes me sick. It's better to keep the three bites down than push myself and throw all of it up."

Rachel looks up from her plate, studying me. "Is there any chance that you could be pregnant?"

"No way. I'm on the pill."

"People get pregnant on the pill, Cait."

Hutch and I were having sex without condoms. A lot. I don't have a clue how many times he came inside me the last week we spent together. But I don't think a pregnancy is at all likely given his history. "I don't think it's physically possible."

"Does he have problems in the erection section?"

I laugh and it's the first time in two weeks. "No. He definitely does not have any problems in the erection section."

"Then why would you think it's not possible?"

It won't hurt anything to tell Rachel the truth. It's not as though she's going to tell anyone. "His wife couldn't get pregnant by him, but she did get pregnant by another man while she was having an affair."

"Did they try to conceive for a long time?"

"She was the one trying... without Hutch's knowledge."

"For real? What a bitch."

Bitch doesn't even begin to cover what Mina was.

"He's not sure how long she was off of her birth control, but it was a while. She was also taking fertility drugs, and she still didn't get pregnant."

"Sounds like he's sterile."

"If he is, I'll never know." Because we aren't going to be together. And even if we were, he doesn't want children.

"I'm sorry about that, Cait. I know how much you love him, but you can't go on living like this. It's not good for you."

"I know. I just need a little more time and it'll be better." It feels like I break a little more each day, but it has to begin to get better at some point, right? I can't still be in this condition a month, six months, or a year from now.

This is day fourteen without being awakened by Hutch's touch, without seeing his handsome face and naughty grin in the morning, without hearing him tell me how much he wants me just one more time before he has to leave the bed and get ready for work.

I love those memories even if they haunt me. I can't regret a single one of them because that would be to wish them away. And I can't do that.

"Classes start tomorrow. That will be a good distraction for you."

"I hope so." I need a diversion, something to break my current train of thought.

I'm sinking slowly and I can't find a way to breathe. My tears are weighing me down, and I don't have the strength or desire to try to make it to the top of the surface for air.

Is it possible to die of a broken heart?

I guess we'll find out.

～

Lease a flat close to campus and pay through the nose for it? Or live farther away, take the train into Edinburgh, and walk twenty minutes to campus? Those were my choices. And because I'm frugal and need this money to last for as long as possible, I'm riding the train—there and back—this and every other day.

I don't mind the train. I can use the time to study or work on my manuscript. Even if it is the story about Hutch and me with one exception: the fiction has a happy ending.

I sit in my seat, waiting for everyone else to leave the early-morning train. I'm in no hurry to fall into that crowd of people rushing to wherever they needed to be five minutes ago. And I'm in no hurry to return to my old life at uni, my life before Hutch.

It's as though my life is moving in reverse instead of going forward. Reverse or forward, both are minus Hutch. And I hate it.

I look at his picture on my phone and stroke my finger over his five-o'clock shadow. It feels nothing like the real thing. His stubbly face would feel so prickly in the morning and then again at the end of the day, especially by the time he came to bed. Oh, how I miss that bristled roughness against my face, my stomach, my inner thighs.

My everything.

I slip my phone into my backpack and leave the train. The knot in my stomach tightens when I pass the spot where Hutch was always waiting for me at Waverley Station. This is the first time he's not there to pick me up. And he never will be again.

My mind has played tug-of-war all day. One minute I'm immersed in whatever the professor has to say, and then the next minute I'm back at the Hutcheson estate with the man I love. And it has to stop. I can't live like this. It's maddening.

I'm on the train again, looking out the window and listening to my favorite playlist—the one I listen to while I write. 'If You Ever Did Believe' by Stevie Nicks is playing. I've always loved the sound of the song, but I don't think I've ever paid much attention to the lyrics until now.

A single tear slides down my cheek and I reach up, wiping it away and hoping that no one sitting around me notices that I'm crying.

I twist my body toward the window when someone takes the seat beside me, and I'm annoyed when that person begins talking to me. Can't you see that I have AirPods in my ears? That's the universal sign meaning that I don't want to talk, asshole. I just want to ride the train in peace.

I jerk my head around, simultaneously removing my AirPod. "I'm sorry. What was that?"

"I said hello, Cait."

No.

No. Fucking. Way.

This isn't happening.

Except it is.

"It's been too long since I've seen you. I've been wondering how you are."

"I'm fine. Great, actually." Cameron glances at the backpack by my feet. "I'm back at uni for my final year."

"I called you on your birthday and then again about a month ago. I spoke to a man. He told me that he was your boyfriend?"

Hutch told Cameron he was my boyfriend?

Why does that make my chest ache so deeply?

"Yeah, he told me about your conversation."

"That's surprising. I didn't think he would."

God, I loved the possessive tone I heard in Hutch's voice when he asked about Cameron. Jealous, even. "He wanted to know who you were and why you were calling me."

"He sounds insecure about your relationship."

"Hutch isn't insecure. He's possessive of what belongs to him. There's a difference."

"You *belong* to him?" Cameron chuckles. "You've never belonged to anyone your entire life, Cait."

I spent a lot of years belonging to no one. And then Hutch claimed me as his. And I let him. I gave him my body and then I gave him my heart. I wanted nothing more than to be his. And I coveted every moment we were together.

"I belonged to him. But it's over now."

"I don't hate to hear that because I have things I need to say to you." Cameron reaches for my hand. "I am truly sorry for what I did to you. You have no idea how much I regret being with that woman. She was the biggest fucking mistake of my life. That one night with her cost me you."

I needed to hear Cameron say these things to me ten months ago. Not that it would have made a difference but it would have made me feel better to hear that he was suffering a little.

"You were my first everything. I gave myself to you because I believed that you loved me, and then the minute my back was turned, you had a one-night stand with another woman. A stranger that you didn't even know. There aren't many things lower than that."

"Everything you're saying is true. I was stupid and it was a mistake."

"I appreciate that you're able to see the wrong in what you did to me."

"Do you think you can forgive me?"

"What you did to me… it hurt. It hurt a lot. But it stopped hurting when I met Hutch, and I forgave you. I forgave you because I no longer cared about what you did to me."

"Does that mean that you no longer care about me or about us?"

He's failing to see that I'm not the same Cait I was ten months ago. "I don't think about us anymore. I haven't in a long time."

"It kills me to hear that because you're all I think about."

There was a time when I would have loved hearing him say that. But not today.

"I don't know what you expect from me."

"I want you, Cait. I didn't realize how much until I didn't have you in my life anymore. I love you."

I love you. My heart has been craving the sound of those three little words. But not from him.

"I'm sorry, Cameron."

"Please, don't close your heart off to me. We can be happy again if you'll give me another chance."

"I can't be happy with you."

"Because of him?"

"Yes. Because of him."

"We have a chance at making us work, but you aren't going to give us another try because you think you still want him?"

"Make no mistake about it. I will always love

him, and I will always want him. That is never going to change."

Ever.

5

MAXWELL HUTCHESON

My memories with Lou—they're everywhere, haunting me day and night. The kitchen. The dining room. The living room. I see her everywhere throughout the house. My bedroom is by far the worst. But my NOLA girl will be back where she belongs soon.

How do I know this? Brady and I finally located Rachel's client, Claud, and he has put me in touch with her. She has agreed to meet tonight. This nightmare is almost over.

"Max, your brother is ringing you. Are you able to take his call?" my secretary asks.

I don't really have time to talk to him right now, but Ian doesn't make a habit of ringing me at work. There must be an important reason for his call. Plus, I haven't forgotten what happened the last time I dodged his calls and texts.

"Aye, put him through, Mary."

"I'm sorry to bother you at work, but I have a

problem, and I need to talk to someone. Can you meet me for lunch?"

Ian is eleven years younger than me. He was still a child when I became a man. As much as I hate it, we aren't close. Never have been. But I wish we were. Perhaps he does too if he's reaching out to me for help with a problem.

"Hold on and give me a second to look at my appointments for today."

Mary sees to it that I have a printout of my appointment schedule on my desk every morning before I arrive at the office. She's very efficient.

"I can meet you at noon."

"Noon would be great."

I'm curious—and troubled—about what's going on with my brother. "Is everything all right?"

"No, Max. Everything is not all right."

"Is there cause for concern?" God, I sound like Mum.

"I'll tell you everything over lunch."

He clearly doesn't want to talk about this over the phone. "Is that new burger place over by uni all right?"

"That works fine."

"I'll see you at noon."

Entering the restaurant an hour later, I take one look at Ian and his face confirms what he said over the phone. Everything is not all right. "You look like shite."

No smart-ass comeback? That's disturbing. It means this is serious. "What's going on?"

Ian runs his hands up and over his face, fisting the top of his hair. "I've fucked up, Max. I've fucked up big time."

"You've only been back at uni for a few days. How badly could you have fucked up in so little time?"

"It didn't just happen." He leans back and rests his head against the back of the bench he's sitting on, banging it a few times. "I hooked up with a girl from uni last semester."

I can tell where this is going. "Please tell me that you have a sexually transmitted disease."

"I wish. Antibiotics would fix that."

"The lass is pregnant?"

"Aye."

"Aww fuck, Ian. Why'd you go and do something like that?"

"Well, I didn't do it on purpose. I don't want a fucking kid."

My wee brother is twenty-two years old. Still a kid himself in so many ways. Not even finished with uni yet. He does not need a baby.

"I don't know what to do."

After my experience, the first thing I'd do is question the paternity. "Are you sure that the bairn is yours?"

"No."

"But you did fuck her?"

"Aye. A few times."

"You used condoms?"

"Every time." He looks away and his voice is low. "Except for once."

Dumb. Fucking. Dobber. "Are you fucking kidding me?"

"I know, I know. It was a stupid mistake. It felt good when I was doing it, but I'm regretting the hell out of it now."

"You said you hooked up with her last semester. How far along does that put her in the pregnancy?"

"All I know is that she's a week away from being too far along to have an abortion."

"Did you discuss abortion with her?"

"I tried but she won't even consider it. She wants to keep the baby, which means I don't get a choice. What part of that is fair to me?"

I understand all too well how my brother is feeling right now. I once had a similar mindset but not anymore. I've come to love Ava Rose and with each passing day I feel more like her father. And I suspect the same would be true for Ian.

"I still have a week to talk her into having an abortion."

I hate to break it to Ian but that's probably a fruit-less hope. "This child has been growing inside of her for months. She has connected with it. The lass isn't likely to change her mind because it's not what you want."

"Then what do I do?"

"If the bairn is yours, you become a father."

"Fuck. Fuck. Fuck!" The final "fuck" barely squeezes through his clenched teeth.

"How do you feel about the girl?"

He shrugs. "She was a great shag. Other than that, I don't really know her."

"Is she pleasant?"

"She's pleasant to look at."

Well, at least there's that. "If there was no bairn, would you consider dating her?"

"Aye, I guess."

"I'm not saying that you ask her to marry you, but I think you should explore a relationship with her. She is going to be your bairn's mother. You don't have to be together to parent this child, but it would make things easier if you were."

"And if things don't work out?" Ian asks.

"You're no worse off for trying, and at least you'll know that you gave it some effort."

"I guess."

"Have you told Mum and Dad?"

He shakes his head. "I've been putting it off. What do you think they'll say?"

"They're going to think that you've been irresponsible, and you have been, but they'll get over it. You know how Mum is about bairns. She'll be happy about getting another one in the family."

"I dread that conversation."

"It may not seem like it right now, but this is eventually going to be all right."

There was a time when being in this same situation would've caused me the same kind of despair but not today. I'm no longer afraid of what life would be like with a family. I'm more afraid of what life without Lou would be like.

She wants babies. If I'm going to make her my wife, I have to give them to her. And I will. As many as she wants, whenever she's ready. By any means.

≈

RACHEL MEGGETT. THE LASS HAS BEEN A KIND, LOYAL friend to Lou and that makes her all right in my book.

She stands when Claud and I enter the parlor. I scan the room, hoping to see Lou, but she isn't here. And my hopes are crushed.

"Mr. Hutcheson. It's a pleasure to see you again."

Rachel and I briefly met the night of the Inamorata gala. We've only shared a few words, but she doesn't feel like a stranger to me. Lou was forever talking about her best friend.

"It's my pleasure. Thank you for agreeing to see me."

"Of course."

Claud goes to the wet bar and picks up a crystal decanter, removing the top. "Would you care for a whisky?"

I've had far too many whiskies the last two weeks. I need to dry out. "I wouldn't care for one but thank you."

Claud and Rachel sit on the sofa, and I take the chair across from them. "You've been in contact with Lou? You told her I was coming?"

"I have and I did."

"Is she all right?"

"Is Cait safe? Yes. Is she all right? No. She's definitely not all right."

She's not all right because she's hurting the same way that I'm hurting?

"She left, disappeared without a word, and she won't respond to my calls or texts."

"I know, but please understand that it hurt her deeply to do so. It's still hurting her."

"What happened? Why did she leave me?"

Rachel sighs, shaking her head. "I can't tell you what happened, but make no mistake about it. She didn't want to leave. It killed her to do so."

"She was forced to leave?" I knew it. I fucking knew it. Lou didn't leave me by choice.

"She won't let me confirm any of the details about

what led to her leaving. I'm only allowed to tell you that she will always love you and Ava Rose."

"I need to see her." I have to make right what Blair has done.

"That's not going to happen."

"Because someone is forcing her to stay away from me." And I know who.

Lou isn't used to dealing with the Lochridges. She can't see that Blair doesn't have the power to hurt her.

"I know Blair threatened Lou the day that she left."

"I can neither confirm nor deny that."

"I don't need you to confirm it." Blair is conniving but not nearly as clever as she believes. "I'm well aware of how my late wife's family operates but Lou isn't. They can't hurt her. You have to tell her that."

"I will, but it won't change anything."

"I want her to come back to me." She has to come back.

"I understand that you enjoyed having Cait as your inamorata, but she isn't coming back."

This isn't how I wanted to do this, but Rachel is my only line of communication to Lou. I have to lay my heart at her feet and hope that she will deliver it to Lou on my behalf.

My chest tightens and my heart hammers against it on the inside. "Lou wasn't an inamorata to me. I love her. I. Love. Her. And I want her back with me where she belongs."

There. I've said it aloud.

A quick breath catches in Rachel's throat. "Hearing that will make her happy, but it's not going to change her mind."

"I love her. She loves me. We should be together."

"I couldn't agree more, but it's more complicated than that."

"All of this is Blair's doing, but I'm going to make it right. She's going to come back to me."

Are those tears in Rachel's eyes?

"Until that time comes, will you please tell her that I love her, and that Ava Rose loves her, and that we miss her terribly?"

"I will tell her."

My nightmare isn't over.

Time to come up with a plan B for dealing with Blair.

6

CAITRIONA LOUDEN

Lou wasn't an inamorata to me. I love her. I. Love. Her. And I want her back with me where she belongs.

I love her. She loves me. We should be together.

She's going to come back to me.

Until that time comes, will you please tell her that I love her, and that Ava Rose loves her, and that we miss her terribly?

Oh my God. He loves me. He really and truly loves me.

Why does hearing that hurt so much?

I cup my hands over my mouth to mute the sound of my sobs so Hutch doesn't hear me. He can't know that I'm in the next room listening to every word he says.

I slide down the wall, becoming a crumpled mess on the floor. And that's how I remain until Hutch leaves and Rachel comes into the room.

"Oh, Ra—" My voice breaks and I'm unable to voice the rest of her name.

She lowers herself to the floor and wraps her

arms around me. "He loves you, Cait. That changes everything."

I shake my head. "It changes nothing."

"You silly lass. How can you possibly say that after hearing him profess his love for you?"

"The world as he knows it will be over if I'm in it. How long do you think he'll continue to love me when my presence in his life means losing everything that he has worked so hard to achieve?"

"If he truly loves you, and I believe that he does, he won't care about what he loses."

"He won't want me if he knows the truth."

"There's only one truth and it's that he loves you. Of course, he wants you. Why would you think otherwise?"

I blink rapidly, trying to force back the tears that are forming a blurry lens over my eyes. "Because I'm pregnant."

The words, even as I hear them come from my own mouth, don't seem real.

"Oh, Cait."

"I don't know how it happened. Even if he's not sterile, which he obviously isn't, I took my pill every day. This shouldn't have happened."

She pulls me against her and squeezes me tightly, igniting a whole new series of sobs. "Are you sure?"

"I haven't seen a doctor yet, but my period is late and the test I took was positive."

"You haven't said a word about it."

"I thought my period was late because my body was thrown off by not eating and sleeping." I never dreamed it was because of a pregnancy.

"It could be a false positive. That happens sometimes."

"Six times?" Because that's how many tests I've taken.

Rachel sucks air though her teeth. "Ooh. That's a lot."

"I have an appointment with a doctor tomorrow."

"What are you going to do if you are?"

"I have no idea."

I've always seen things differently in my mind when I imagined what it would be like to find out that I was going to be a mother. My baby would be the long-awaited answer to a prayer. My husband would be thrilled and walking on air. But neither of those things is the case.

The reality is that Maxwell Hutcheson may love me, but he will not be happy about a baby. He's made his feelings about it very clear. And that shatters my heart into a million pieces.

I may not be able to have Hutch for myself, but I'll always have a piece of him. That brings me a little bit of happiness.

I'm sitting on the exam table waiting for the doctor. I realize how hard I'm gripping the edge when I notice my blanched knuckles. I bet my face doesn't look much different.

"Stop fidgeting. You're making me nervous."

Did Rachel really just say that I'm the one making her nervous? "Oh, I'm sorry. I wouldn't want you to be nervous or anything since it's you sitting up here on this exam table about to find out if you're pregnant or not."

Rachel flips to the next page in the magazine she's

looking at. "You took six tests and every one of them was positive. Are you really still holding out hope that you're not pregnant?"

She's right. Six positive pregnancy tests can't all be wrong. But a girl can hope.

"Let me live in my world of denial for just a little while longer, okay?"

"Okay. If that's what you want… Mummy."

The door opens and my doctor comes into the room. "Good morning, Miss Louden. How are you doing today?"

"That all depends upon what you tell me."

Butterflies dance in my stomach and my heart beats out of my chest while I await the verdict.

"You're pregnant."

My face suddenly feels cold, yet I feel flashes of heat, and my head spins.

Rachel reaches out and grips my arm when I sway a little. "Cait! Are you okay?"

No. I'm not at all okay. "I need to lie down."

I twist, lowering myself to lie on my side on the exam table.

"Slow, deep breaths," the doctor says.

Woozy. Short of breath despite my gasps for air. Spots in front of my eyes. "I think I'm going to pass out."

"Listen to me. You're hyperventilating. Slow your breathing, and you'll feel better."

I do as my doctor says, taking slower breaths. After a few moments, I begin to feel like things are returning to normal. "I think I'm better now."

"Are you sure? You still don't look right to me," Rachel says.

I hold out my hand, watching it tremble. "I'm as good as I'm going to be."

My doctor offers her hand. "Let's see how you tolerate sitting up."

She pulls on my hand and grips the back of my shoulder, helping me to sit. "We need to figure out how far along you are. When was your last period?"

I don't remember the date off the top of my head. "I need to look at a calendar."

Rachel takes out her phone and holds it up, showing me a calendar.

"August twelfth." I remember now because I was so happy it wasn't happening the last two weeks Hutch and I were together.

My doctor twists a plastic wheel in her hand. "That places your pregnancy at six weeks and a day, making you due on May 19th. Does that sound right?"

"I guess so."

"We should do an ultrasound to confirm your dates and make sure that the fetus is developing as it should. Let me check with radiology and see when they can work you in."

Pregnancy. Due date. Ultrasound.

This isn't happening. This isn't happening. This isn't happening.

Except it is.

Rachel comes to me and wraps her arms around me. And that's when the tears begin. "Shh. Stop that now. This is going to be all right."

"In what world is this going to be all right?"

"I don't know. It just sounded like the right thing to say."

In the back of my mind, I still had hope that my

relationship with Hutch could somehow work out. I didn't know how. I only knew that a small flicker of hope was still burning. And now it's not.

Hutch has worked hard and has warmed up to the idea of being a father to Ava Rose. I'm proud of how far he's come, but he still has a long way to go. How can I ask him to do it all over again with another unwanted child?

I don't think he can bear it.

The nurse returns to the exam room a few minutes later. "Radiology has to work you into the schedule, so it could be a while. You have time to call the baby's father if you want him to be with you during the ultrasound."

Absolutely not. "My friend is going to be with me."

She opens a drawer and takes out a sheet. "Remove your bottoms and wrap this around your waist. A tech should be with you soon to do your scan."

Naked from the waist down, my body trembles as I lie on the exam table. Rachel pats my arm. "Are you cold?"

"No."

"Nervous?"

"Very."

"I wish I knew what to say to make this better. but I can't think of anything."

Words aren't what I need right now. "Your being here with me makes it better. I don't know what I'd do if I was alone."

"I would never let you do this alone. But what about Hutch?"

"He isn't going to want any part of this."

"You don't know that."

I do know that. "He's already had one child forced upon him that he didn't want. How do you think that he'll feel about another one?"

"This is an entirely different situation. He loves you and this baby belongs to him. He has the right to know about it."

I would never keep anything so important from him. "I'm going to tell him about it, but I need time. I'm not ready yet."

I lie on the exam table, imagining everything about this baby. Is it a boy? A girl? Will it be tall like Hutch or short like me? Will it have my hazel eyes? Or Hutch's pale blues? I hope for the latter. His eyes are beautiful.

The door opens and a woman that I assume is the ultrasound tech comes into the room, rolling a large machine behind her. "Miss Louden?"

I rise to a sitting position and straighten my sheet. "Yes."

"I'm Diana and I'm going to be doing your ultrasound."

She sits on the stool beside me and taps on the keyboard of the ultrasound machine. "Based upon your last menstrual period, it looks like you're around six weeks along?"

"That's what Dr. Kimble told me."

The tech adjusts the sheet and squeezes a generous amount of warm gel on my stomach. She presses the wand against my lower belly, rocking it back and forth. "I'll take measurements of your uterus first."

I stare at the ceiling, wishing all of this would go away.

"Don't you want to look?" Rachel asks.

I don't think I can without losing it entirely. "No."

The tech pushes harder against my stomach. "Ah, there he is. He was hiding from us."

Opening my eyes, I jerk my head around and look at the screen. "I want to see it."

Reaching out, she touches the monitor. "This little white dot is your baby."

How can a little white dot be a baby? "Are you sure?"

"Positive," she says.

"Everything looks normal?"

"It's still very early but all looks well from what I can see today. The baby appears to be growing right on schedule."

I'm entranced by the white oblong circle on the screen, the beginning of a tiny human being. A baby that Hutch and I came together and created.

Part of him.

Part of me.

Our baby.

The ultrasound tech tears off a printout from the machine and hands it to me. "All done. You can get dressed now."

"Thank you."

"You're welcome. Congratulations and best wishes."

Congratulations and best wishes? That makes all of this feel far too real.

Rachel gets up and fetches my clothes, holding them out for me. "You're eating for two now. I think you need a big cheeseburger and some beer-battered onion rings."

Grease. The thought of it makes me want to hurl. "I'll pass."

"You've barely eaten enough to keep a bird alive. You need to put some nutrients in your body for the baby."

I know Rachel is right.

"Pick a place."

"Tigerlily."

This is her way of bribing me to eat. She knows that I can't resist their chicken-and-bacon club sandwich. "Tigerlily sounds really good right now."

∾

THE SERVER PLACES OUR FOOD ON THE TABLE. "ENJOY and let me know if you need anything else."

"Thank you."

I wasn't sure that I would be able to eat, but I feel hungry for the first time in weeks now that my favorite sandwich is in front of me. "This looks really good."

"I thought that sandwich might entice your appetite to return."

"Thanks for bribing me into coming."

"You have a bairn to look after now. Going without food is over."

It's nice to have someone looking out for me. "I have to eat for the baby and I understand that."

"May 19th feels like forever away, but it isn't. The baby will be here before you know it."

I wonder when graduation will be. It has to be sometime around my due date. "At least I'll be able to finish classes before I give birth." Unless something happens and I deliver early.

"Would you be mad at me if I told you that I'm excited about the bairn?"

"I wouldn't be mad but I'd wonder why you were excited."

"Because you're going to have a wee one. It'll be so adorable. And so much fun."

I wish I could feel like Rachel. "You should be the one having a baby."

"I wish I was."

"Do you really mean that?"

"I do. I would love to be a mum."

"What does Claud have to say about that?"

"He wants a child. And at forty-four, he doesn't want to wait much longer."

Sounds as though they're having some serious discussions about it. "Lucky you."

"You don't know for sure that Hutch doesn't want this child."

I clear my throat. "'I lack the gene that drives a man to want to father a child.' Those were his exact words. And you've not seen the way he struggles with being a father to Ava Rose. He works at it, but it's an uphill battle all of the way for him."

"If he's so opposed to parenthood, do you think he'd ask you to have an abortion?"

I swallow my food and think about that for a second. "I hadn't even considered that possibility."

"I know how much you love him so if he asked, would you consider doing it?"

I'm in shock about this pregnancy, but I want this baby. "I would never consider abortion. If he doesn't want to be a part of this baby's life, he doesn't have to be. I can raise it on my own."

"You're the strongest person I know, so I don't

doubt that for a second. When are you going to tell him?"

"I think I should wait at least a couple of weeks. Let me come to grips with it before I try to tell him." Because quite honestly, I don't know what in the world I'll say.

"I think the baby negates all of the ultimatums of the sister-in-law."

"What do you mean?"

"You're having Maxwell Hutcheson's baby. That's a truth that is going to come out. Her threats about exposing your relationship seem null to me."

"I hadn't thought of it that way, but you're right. She lost her leverage when I became pregnant."

"Would he ask you to not name him as the father?"

"I don't think so." And if he did, it would break my heart all over again.

"I think this baby is going to bring you back together."

"Don't say that." Hearing things like that makes me get my hopes up.

"After talking with him last night, I believe it will for sure. He loves you so much, and I think he's going to surprise you with how he takes this news."

Is it possible? Could Hutch want this baby?

I'm afraid to hope.

7

MAXWELL HUTCHESON

LOU LOVES ME. SHE DIDN'T LEAVE OF HER OWN ACCORD. So what the fuck could Blair possibly be holding over Lou's head? And why is she allowing Blair to control her actions?

I can't figure it out. The only thing I'm certain of is that Lou won't see me until I take care of this with Blair.

I've been racking my brain for ideas since I saw Rachel two nights ago. I've come up with nothing.

I'm on my fifth whisky of the night. Maybe sixth. Doesn't matter what number you put on it—it's the one that makes being in this house without Lou bearable.

I turn up the last of my whisky and see the figure of a woman over the glass.

Lou?

My elation quickly turns to anger when my eyes focus and I register who it is. "Blair. I was just thinking about you."

She smiles. "You know how to make a woman feel special."

I sit taller and slide toward the coffee table, pouring myself another whisky. "Grab a glass from the bar and have a drink with me."

She places the glass on the table in front of me, and I pour four fingers high. "What brings you all the way out to Kirkliston?"

"You were upset the last time I saw you. I wanted to check in and see how you were doing."

I hold up my whisky glass. "I'm fucking miserable. That's how I'm doing."

It's such a kick in the bollocks to find happiness after two years of misery and then have it ripped out of your life.

"Why are you miserable?"

That fucking faux innocent tone in her voice makes me want to rip out her vocal cords.

"You know very well why."

"For the life of me, I don't know."

"Lou is gone and you're the reason."

"She told you that?"

"Lou has told me nothing because I've not seen her since the day she walked out of here without so much as a goodbye. And she refuses to see me."

Blair does a shitty job of hiding her satisfaction. "And that is somehow my fault?"

"I believe it is."

"Why would I do anything to make your house-keeper leave her position?"

"Stop being coy. It doesn't suit you. We both know that she isn't my housekeeper."

Blair shrugs and shakes her head. "I don't know what you're talking about."

This game she's playing is infuriating.

"Lou and I were having an affair. You knew. And you didn't like it worth a damn."

Blair breathes in deeply and slowly releases the air. "That woman, that whore, has no place in your life or Ava Rose's."

"Lou isn't a whore. But even if she was, it wouldn't be your place to decide who is or isn't in my life."

"Mina wouldn't want a prostitute living under the same roof as her daughter."

"Lou isn't a prostitute."

"She is according to my sources."

Blair has *sources*. Okay. This is starting to come together now. "Who are your sources?"

"A very reputable private investigator. And also the son of Inamorata's owner."

Chambers. I knew that bastard would find a way to hurt Lou.

"You know nothing about Lou."

"She's an escort and you paid her to have sex with you. That's the definition of a prostitute."

Well, fuck. That much is true. And it sounds bad when she says it like that.

"How could you think that bringing that woman into your home would be acceptable?"

"This is my house and what I do here is my business. I don't owe you an explanation about anything I do in the privacy of my own home."

"You do as long as Ava Rose lives in this house. And if at any time your actions become unfit, it's my job to step in and help you find your way back onto the right path."

So Blair has made herself the warden who governs my actions? Let's see what she has to say about this.

"I love Lou."

There's a catch in her throat and her eyes widen. "No. That can't happen."

"Too late. It already has."

"Don't say that."

"I. Love. Lou."

"You can't love someone else. It'll ruin everything."

"What will it ruin?"

"Do you really not see the truth of what's been happening all these years?"

The only truth that I know about all of these years is that getting tied up with the Lochridges has led me down a road of misery and despair. "What truth?"

"You shouldn't have married Mina."

I couldn't agree more, but I can't believe that I'm hearing that out of Blair. "No truer words have ever been spoken."

Blair places her glass on the table and gets up, walking over and standing in front of me.

What the fuck is she doing?

"I always saw your true worth. Mina never did."

She unties the belt at her waist, opening her wrap dress to reveal her naked body beneath. Lifting one of her legs, she moves to climb on top of me but I reach out, gripping her waist. "No. Don't do that."

"I know you want me. You always have."

I don't know what in the fuck I could have done to give Blair that impression. "You're wrong. Very wrong."

She drops to her knees in front of me and reaches for my belt buckle. "I've always wondered what it would feel like to have you in my mouth."

I push at her hands, but her grip around my buckle is tight. "Stop. Now."

She stops tugging on my belt, but her grip doesn't lessen. "Let me see if I have this right. I'm trying to suck you off and you're telling me no?"

"That is accurate."

"You're turning down a blowjob from me?"

How many different ways does she need to hear rejection? "I don't want you to blow me."

Blair's laughter clearly isn't sparked by humor. "You're rejecting me because of this nobody whore who calls herself Lou?"

"I love her." And her lips are the only ones I want wrapped around my cock.

"You can't be serious."

"I've never been more serious in my life."

"You have to know that I'll never let you be with her."

It's laughable that she truly believes she has the right to say how I live my life.

"You can't stop me from being with her."

"If you bring that whore back into your life, I will ruin you. I will tell Dad everything."

"Go ahead. Tell him that I'm in love with Lou. Tell him that I want to make her my wife. Tell him to fire me and ensure that I never work in Edinburgh again. The three of us will be happier in Glasgow anyway."

Aye, it's a dick move to threaten Blair with moving Ava Rose to Glasgow, but what choice has she given me?

"Try to take my niece out of Edinburgh, and you'll find out what happens when you fuck with the Lochridges."

"Ava Rose is my daughter. I can take her anywhere I want."

A grin of pure evil spreads across Blair's face. "Come on, Max. We both know that Ava Rose is not your daughter."

Whoa.

Wait a fucking minute.

Blair knows?

It feels like someone has knocked the breath right out of me. "What are you talking about?"

"You think my sister didn't confide in me?"

It's hard for me to believe that Mina would have confided in Blair about anything. Of her three sisters, Blair was her least favorite.

"I don't know what Mina told you, but I think you're confused."

"Of the two of us, I'm the only one who isn't confused about the truth. I know everything about Mina's affair and who fathered Ava Rose."

She knows who got Mina pregnant?

I've never wanted to know who Ava Rose's father is. Being unaware meant not carrying the burden of withholding her from her true paternal family. Learning the truth would change everything.

"Don't tell me who he is. I don't want to know."

"Don't worry. I don't plan on telling you or him unless I have no other choice."

The biological father doesn't know about Ava Rose. That's good to know.

"What do you mean by no other choice?"

"If you choose to bring Lou back into your life, it'll mean losing custody of Ava Rose. I'll tell everyone that you aren't her biological father, and a paternity test will prove it. There won't be a judge in Edinburgh who would rule for her to remain in the care of a man who isn't her father rather than placing her with her real family."

"You'd do that to her? And to me? Take her away from the only parent she's ever known?"

"I wouldn't want to, but you'd be leaving me with no choice if you choose to have Caitriona Louden in your life."

Lou's real name is Caitriona Louden.

Finally, I have a name for her.

"You'd make me choose between my daughter and the woman I love?"

"I certainly would, but there's another option to consider."

"What other option?"

"We could raise Ava Rose together as our daughter."

Our daughter? Mine and Blair's?

What the actual fuck?

"Are you suggesting that we share custody?"

"No, Max. I want you to marry me. I want to be Ava Rose's mother. And your wife."

That's the craziest shite I've ever heard. "You're already married."

"I can begin the divorce process tomorrow."

My brother-in-law Doug. The poor bastard has no idea that his wife has come to my house, gotten on her knees and tried to suck my cock, and told me she wants to divorce him and marry me.

"Yer aff yer heid if you think that I'd ever marry you."

Blair sits back, her bum against her lower legs. "You'll marry me or lose everything you love. Your choice."

I've already lost everything I love.

"Get out. Now."

Blair stands and adjusts her dress, retying the belt around her waist. "I want you, Max. And for that reason, I'm going to give you time to think about what I'm offering you."

I don't need time to think about anything. "No deal."

"You shouldn't make your decision in haste. Make no mistake about it. The price of having Caitriona is high. It's a price that you can't afford."

If she were a man, I'd punch her in her fucking face.

"Go home to your husband." The poor fool.

I forgo the tumbler and turn up the bottle of whisky. The liquid scorches my throat all the way until it hits my gut, and then the fire spreads inside of my core.

Without doubt, Blair is the spawn of Thomas Lochridge. And she may actually be eviler than her father is.

Ava Rose. I have come to love that little girl so much. And I could lose her if Lou comes back into my life.

My daughter or the woman I love? How do I make that kind of choice?

I can't. There has to be another way. I can't lose either of them. I won't.

I find the bottom of the bottle quickly and opt to sleep on the couch. I don't want another repeat of today—waking to a cold bed and reaching out only to find an empty space beside me.

"Come back to me, Lou. Come. Back. Please."

8

CAITRIONA LOUDEN

TWO WEEKS LATER

ANOTHER RESTLESS NIGHT. THAT'S MY NIGHTLY RITUAL despite the exhaustion I constantly feel. This pregnancy has robbed me of all my energy. But that's normal at this stage according to everything I've read.

I lie on my back, staring at the darkness dancing on my bedroom ceiling. It's my other nightly routine and has been for almost six weeks. It's hard to believe that my separation from Hutch is approaching the month-and-a-half mark.

I've somehow managed to survive without him. Not that I really wanted to in the beginning but this baby has changed everything. I already love our child with all of my heart.

I haven't felt well today. It's been the worst day so far. My stomach has been threatening to send me to the toilet for hours, and it finally makes good on its threats.

Sudden. Sharp. Stabbing.

My abdomen hasn't cramped like this in years.

Not since I was a teenager and having trouble with my periods and menstrual cramps.

Bright. Red. Blood. A lot of it.

What is this? What is happening?

I wipe away the blood and more replaces it. "Nooo!"

No, no, no. This isn't happening. I'm not losing this baby.

Drip. Drip. Drip.

More blood.

"Oh God, no."

Tucking a towel between my legs, I return to bed and call Rachel.

"What's wrong?"

"I need you to come over and take me to the hospital." I feel a huge gush between my legs. "I'm bleeding."

"How badly?"

"It's a lot."

"All right. We'll be right there."

I lie motionless on my back, crying, as I wait for Rachel to arrive. I'm terrified that any kind of movement could be the single motion that causes me to lose this baby.

That can't happen. I lost Hutch. I can't lose his baby too. The pain will be too much to bear.

A thin sheen of sweat has formed over my body, and I'm trembling when Rachel and Claud come into my bedroom.

"Tell me what's happening."

"My lower abdomen is cramping and I'm bleeding. A lot."

Rachel lifts the covers and pulls back the towel between my legs. "You need to see a doctor."

Rachel motions for Claud to come to us. "Carry her to the car."

"It's bad, isn't it?" I haven't looked but I felt it coming out.

Three heartbeats pass before Rachel answers. "It's a lot."

Claud pushes his arms beneath me and lifts my body from the bed, the movement making my cramp intensify tenfold. "Ohh, it hurts."

"I'm sorry," Claud says.

I wrap my arms around his shoulders and as tightly as I can in spite of the weakness overtaking my body. "I'm losing the baby. I know I am."

"We're going to do everything possible to make sure that you don't."

Something is coming out of me down there, but I can't bring myself to say the words. Admitting it makes the possibility too real.

Rachel covers me with a blanket and Claud carries me to the lift. And I pray with every step that God will allow this tiny little baby to remain inside of me.

Please, please, please don't take this baby from me. I want to be its mother so badly. I want to love it. And I want it to love me.

Claud gently places me in the back seat and Rachel crawls in beside me. She lifts my head, placing it in her lap, and strokes the top of my head. "It's going to be okay, Caity bug."

I don't say the words but I think Rachel is wrong. There's too much blood for everything to be okay.

"I know what you're thinking but this baby is a part of you. I've never known a stronger person in my life. This baby is going to be okay."

Claud's driver makes a turn and I grip my stomach. "Ohhh," I hiss through my clenched teeth.

"I'm sorry. He's just trying to hurry."

"It's not his driving. The pain is getting worse on its own whether I'm jostled or not."

The bright lights of the hospital's glowing sign are a welcome sight. But I think we're too late.

"Don't move. I'll go inside to get someone," Claud says.

Rachel is still stroking the top of my head when Claud returns to the car with two staff members of the hospital and a wheelchair.

"Are you able to move?" one of the nurses asked.

"Probably not quickly, but yes, I think I can move."

Rachel helps me sit up and scoot toward the open door. The staff members grasp me beneath my arms and assist me to the wheelchair. The drenched towel drops to the ground and I see the proof of how heavily I'm bleeding.

I'm taken to an exam room and assessed by a couple of hospital staff members, nurses I presume. One asks me a million questions while the other takes my vital signs and a third appears and draws blood.

"The first thing Dr. Kimble will want to do is an ultrasound to evaluate what's going on."

Oh God. This is it. Someone is going to swirl that wand around my stomach and tell me if my baby is gone from my body.

"Will I have to wait long?"

"Someone should be in very soon."

The nurses step out of the exam room, leaving me alone with Rachel.

"On the way to the hospital, I felt something come out."

A soft gasp catches in Rachel's throat. "You didn't tell me that."

"I couldn't bring myself to say the words."

Rachel reaches for my hand. "Ohhh, Cait."

My chest aches. "I think I've lost the only piece of Hutch that I had left."

Rachel laces her fingers through mine, entwining our hands. "You must have faith, Cait."

"I want to." But that's a very difficult thing to have when you've known nothing but heartache your entire life.

Good things don't happen to me. Choose the worst possible outcome and that's my fate. And losing my child feels like the next tragedy waiting to happen.

The door opens and my doctor comes into the room. Behind her is a woman rolling an ultrasound machine and I know exactly what to expect this time.

"Hello, Caitriona. The nurses tell me that you've come in because you're having pain and bleeding."

"I am."

"When did this start?"

"I had mild cramping earlier today. I thought it was stomach cramps, but then the pain got a lot worse and there was blood when I went to the toilet."

"When did the bleeding start?"

"About an hour ago."

"We're going to do an ultrasound and find out what's happening."

Warm gel on my skin and a wand pressed against my lower belly. I thought I was scared to death when we did this same thing two weeks ago but tonight I feel a completely different kind of fear.

I hold my breath, waiting for Dr. Kimble to tell me the fate of my son or daughter's life. And every moment between the beats of my heart feels like an hour rather than a second.

I suck air between my teeth when Dr. Kimble presses the wand against my lower right side.

"That area is tender?"

"Yes. Very." And it's new. I wasn't tender there earlier.

"I'm sorry. I know this is uncomfortable. I'll try to not press harder than necessary."

"It's fine. Press as hard as you need to."

Dr. Kimble twists a knob on the machine, and I hear a fast and steady swooshing.

"That's your baby's heartbeat."

I look at Rachel, my mouth open, but I can't form any words. Only tears.

"What a beautiful sound, Cait."

"The most beautiful sound I've ever heard." My voice breaks on the last word.

Dr. Kimble finishes the ultrasound and rolls her stool over so she's facing me. "We have a problem, Caitriona."

The happiness and hope in my heart immediately plummet.

"The good news. Your baby has a heartbeat so you've not miscarried, but you do have a subchorionic bleed between the uterus and the placenta. And it's a big one."

"That sounds serious."

"Most of these kinds of bleeds will stop, and the hematoma will dissolve on its own without any kind of intervention. But occasionally the bleeding doesn't stop, and the placenta will separate from the uterine wall. The pregnancy ends in a miscarriage when that happens."

"Is that what's happening to me?"

"It could be."

"Am I going to lose my baby?"

"It could go either way at this point."

Words can't describe the fear I feel inside.

"Is there anything that can be done to save my baby?" I will do anything that might swing the pendulum in our favor.

"The bleeding needs to stop, and the only thing that could help with that at this point is bed rest."

"I'll do whatever you want me to."

"I wish all of my patients were as compliant as you."

"I just want what's best for my baby."

Please survive this, little baby.

Please.

9

MAXWELL HUTCHESON

I WAS THRILLED WHEN RACHEL CALLED AND ASKED TO meet. I was so certain that she had good news. But after seeing her face, I can tell that something isn't right. "What is wrong?"

"Oh God." Rachel cups her hand over her forehead and turns away. "Cait may hate me forever for doing this." Her voice is low as though she may be talking to herself rather than me.

"I doubt that. She doesn't have it in her to hate anyone." Not even the bastards who have mistreated her.

Rachel's face scrunches and she looks upward, blinking rapidly. "I don't know how to say this to you without crying."

Okay. Now she's scaring the shite out of me. "Is Lou all right?"

Rachel shakes her head and a pair of tears fall down her cheeks. "She isn't all right. She needs you now more than ever."

Countless terrifying scenarios rush through my mind. "What has happened?"

"I'm not the one who should be telling you this. I don't know how to say it to you." Rachel squeezes her eyes shut, and more tears roll down her cheeks.

She can't throw something like that out there and then not tell me what's going on. "I need you to just say it. I'm imagining the worst right now."

"Cait was pregnant with your baby but she miscarried." Rachel's chest vibrates when she inhales deeply. "She's devastated and not handling it well."

It's not often that someone has the capability of shaking me to the core, but I am officially shaken. And speechless.

A baby? *My* baby?

I thought I couldn't have children.

Was I wrong all of this time?

"She was going to tell you about the baby after the shock wore off. But she didn't get the chance because she started having complications."

Medical complications typically mean danger. "What kind of complications? Is she going to be okay?"

"The miscarriage didn't happen quickly. She had pain and bleeding, a lot of bleeding, for days. She hemorrhaged and had to have emergency surgery. I don't even know how many bags of blood they had to give her."

"Is she still in the hospital?"

"They released her yesterday."

"When did this happen?"

"It all started a week ago, and it's been four days since she lost the baby." Rachel inhales deeply. "She's a wreck. You can't imagine how much she wanted that baby. It was the only part of you that she had left, and losing it has devastated her."

Lou is hurting and I can't stand it. I don't want her to ever feel pain. "I have to see her."

"I was praying you'd feel that way, but you need to hear the rest of the story before you see her. The part about your sister-in-law. The part you're not supposed to ever know."

"What did Blair do to her?"

"Your sister-in-law hired a private investigator. She knows everything about your inamorata-client arrangement. She threatened to ruin you if Cait didn't leave. The only reason she complied was because she loves you and couldn't bear to be the cause of your downfall."

And like always, Blair got what she wanted. Zero surprise there. "I suspected as much."

"Everything Cait did was out of love for you."

"I'm not angry with Lou. I just want her back." Being together again is the only thing that matters to me at this point.

"I've seen Cait hurt before but never like this. And I can't help her. You're the only one who can make her pain better."

"Take me to her."

Forty-six days. That's how long it's been since I've seen Lou's beautiful face. Since I've heard her contagious laughter. Since I've held her in my arms.

Forty-six days. And I died a wee bit each day she wasn't in my life.

Thank fuck it won't be forty-seven.

My heart is pounding erratically and throbbing in my ears when Calvin stops the car in front of Lou's building. And I can't believe it. She's been living only ten miles away from me. I've driven by her building countless times since she left. But ten miles might as well have been ten thousand when I had no idea where she was.

Rachel lets me into the flat and I enter Lou's bedroom. And all of the time that separated us disappears when I see her lying on her side, sleeping with one hand tucked beneath the side of her face. I don't know how many times I've awakened and seen her just like that. And I miss it desperately. But never again.

I kick out of my shoes and pull back the covers, slipping beneath them. I inch closer until my front presses against her back and I wrap my arm around her middle section.

"Mo maise," I whisper.

She twitches and I pull her closer, pressing my nose against the back of her hair and inhaling deeply.

"Mo maise," I say again, this time a wee bit louder than a whisper.

"Hutch?" Her voice is hoarse and my name is barely decipherable.

"Aye. I'm here."

"This feels real. Not like the other dreams I've had."

"This is real."

"The medicine does weird things to me, but I take it because it helps me forget what happened." Her voice remains dazed as though she might still be lingering between sleep and wake.

"Look at me, Lou. I'm here with you."

She twists and looks at me over her shoulder for a moment before turning over and wrapping her arms around me. She squeezes tightly, pulling me against her.

"I've got you, my sweet lass, and everything is going to be all right. I promise."

She pulls away and looks at me, her eyes taking a moment to focus on mine. "You really are here."

"I am."

Her hand wraps around my cheek, cradling it. "Something terrible has happened."

"I know."

"I was pregnant… but I lost the baby."

"I know."

"I was going to tell you. I swear I was but—"

She presses her forehead to mine and her body shudders. She sucks in a quick, deep breath, and then a sob that possesses the power of ripping your heart apart fills the room.

"I'm so sorry you went through that without me. I wish I'd been with you."

Her tears trigger mine, and together, we grieve for the bairn we've lost. I mourn the passing of a child who was gone before I ever knew it existed. My heart bleeds for a wee one I didn't know I wanted until now.

The pain. The sorrow. The longing.

It's real.

Lou struggles to catch her breath. "I wanted our baby. Words aren't enough to tell you how much I wanted our son or daughter. And it feels like I've lost a piece of my heart."

I hold her against me, stroking the back of her hair. "I know I haven't given you a reason to think so but I would have been happy about the baby."

She lifts her face and her eyes connect with mine. "I thought you wouldn't want it."

"I love you, Lou. How could I not want a child who is a part of you?"

"Hearing you say that makes me happy and sad at the same time."

This lost child will always be in Lou's heart, but there will come a time when she will be ready to try again. She doesn't know it yet but I want to give her another baby. Babies. As many babies as she wants.

I grasp the sides of her face. "We've lost something very special, and it's extraordinarily painful, but we will get through this together."

She nods and our heads move in synchronization. "I'm going to cling to you with everything I have because only your love and strength can pull me through this."

I don't know how long we lie there holding one another, saying nothing, yet speaking to each other in a silent language we both understand. Every breath, every touch tells me how much she loves me.

But I have words to say to her. Important words.

I caress my fingertips down her upper arm. "I love you, Lou. I love you so much."

She lifts her face and looks at me. "I love you too. And I didn't want to go. Blair forced me to do it."

"Rachel told me everything. But even before she did, I already knew Blair was somehow responsible for your leaving."

"She says I'm not fit to be in Ava Rose's life, but that woman is the one who is vile."

Vile is too kind a word to describe Blair. "She's trying to blackmail me into marrying her."

"Marrying her? Isn't she already married?"

"She has this insane idea that she will divorce her husband, and then she and I will marry and raise Ava Rose as our daughter."

"You can't marry that woman." Is that panic in Lou's voice? Does she really believe that I would ever consider that?

"I would choose death over being married to another Lochridge woman. But she has backed me into a corner, and I'm not sure what I'm going to do."

Now is the wrong time to be having this conversation. We should be mourning the loss of our child, not planning our line of defense against Blair.

"We don't have to talk about her right now. You need to rest and recover."

"I can't rest until I know what she's up to."

No, I don't suppose she can rest with so much hanging in the air. "Blair knows that I'm not Ava Rose's biological father. She's threatening to take her away from me if I don't do what she wants—marry her and never see you again."

Lou looks as though she's allowing that to soak in for a moment. "She's threatening to take a baby away from the only parent she's ever known as a ploy to get what she wants? How can anyone be so evil?"

Lou is shocked, but I'm not. There are no limits to what the Lochridges will do. "They will use any means necessary to cut down anyone who is standing in the way of what they want."

"She knows who fathered Ava Rose?"

"She claims to know."

"Do you think she's telling the truth?"

"Unfortunately, I do." The Lochridges aren't known for making empty threats. "She could talk him into coming forward and claiming Ava Rose as his daughter."

"You've been raising her since she was born. You're the only father she's ever known. He can't just come forward and take her from you."

No, but he can petition for custody.

"I have an appointment with a solicitor next week." And I'm terrified to find out what my rights may or may not be. "I love that wee lass. I can't lose her."

Lou rolls away from me and lies on her back, looking up at the ceiling. "I can't be the reason you lose your daughter. I wouldn't be able to get over that and neither would you."

Blair is clever, using Lou's tender heart and love for me as a weapon against her. But I see what she's doing. And it isn't going to work. "Let's get one thing straight right now. You are mine, Lou, and I won't lose you over this."

"You're going to lose one of us. She's going to make sure that happens."

"She isn't going to win. I won't let her."

Lou's eyes are filled with doubt and I can understand why. I don't have a strategy for fixing this shite storm. It's going to take time to come up with a concrete plan.

"Do you want to see Ava Rose?"

"Of course, I want to see her. Will you go get her?"

"Better than that. I'll have Mrs. McVey pack her bag and bring her to us." I knew that would bring a smile to her face.

"Call her now. Please. I haven't seen her since the day I left. I can't wait another minute."

Lou showers while we wait for Ava Rose to arrive. She's exhausted by the time she finishes, and her plan to move to the couch is thwarted.

Lou's so pale and weak. But I'm going to take care of her and nurse her back to health.

Her eyes sparkle, or maybe glisten with tears, when she sees Ava Rose for the first time in forty-six days. "There she is. My sweet girl."

She repositions the pillows behind her back and reaches out for Ava Rose. I lower her into her arms and she cradles her like a mum holding her newborn baby for the first time. And Ava Rose lets her. "She has grown so much since I last saw her. I can't believe how much she has changed. It sort of breaks my heart."

I was worried that Ava Rose would fret because she wouldn't remember Lou, but that clearly isn't the case. I see the eye contact between them, and I know that Ava Rose hasn't forgotten Lou at all. "She remembers you."

"I was afraid she wouldn't."

Lou brings Ava Rose's chubby hand to her mouth and kisses the top. "I've missed you so much, my little carrot top."

Ava Rose steals all of Lou's attention, and I'm perfectly all right with that. My daughter makes her happy. She eases Lou's suffering.

I lie beside them, watching the two of them together again. And I know in my heart that this picture—Lou, Ava Rose, and me as a family—is how things are supposed to be.

10

CAITRIONA LOUDEN

I STARE AT THE CEILING TILES AND HUTCH HOLDS MY hand while Dr. Kimble does my pelvic exam.

"Things look good down here and your blood work is normal, which is surprising. I thought you'd still be anemic. Have you had a cycle yet?"

"I had a light period last week."

"Very good."

Dr. Kimble removes the vagina-opener thing and pulls the sheet down to cover my lower body. After removing her gloves, she offers her hand and pulls me into to a sitting position. She always does that when she wants to talk.

"You can resume sexual activity. Do you want a prescription for birth control or are you planning to try to conceive again?"

Hutch and I haven't talked about it, but a conversation like that isn't necessary. I already know that we won't be trying to conceive. "I need birth control."

"Do you want to go back to the pill or try something new?"

I got pregnant on the pill and I was taking it correctly. My level of trust in it is zero. "I want something different."

"A lot of my patients like the vaginal ring. They especially like that they don't have to think about it on a daily basis. Would that be of interest?"

I like the idea of not setting a daily reminder to take care of birth control. "I'm open to giving it a try."

"You'll obviously need to use a backup birth control method for a month, but I'm sure you know that already."

"Yes."

"Continue taking your vitamins and iron until the prescription runs out." Dr. Kimble holds out my new birth-control prescription. "Do you have any questions?"

"I think you answered most of them at my last appointment." I turn and look at Hutch. "Do you have any questions?"

I think the one he had on his mind has already been answered.

He shakes his head. "I can't think of anything."

I love Dr. Kimble. She's been so kind and understanding during this time, always reassuring me that my miscarriage was no fault of mine and not an indicator of problems with future pregnancies. And that's something that I needed to hear. It's something that I needed to hear more than once.

When we're in the car, Hutch laces his fingers through mine, bringing our clasped hands to rest on his thigh. "It's a relief to hear that you're healthy again."

It's taken six weeks plus a lot of vitamins and iron supplements for my strength to return. "I finally feel like my old self again."

"You have your spark back. And your color."

I'm happy about that. I looked like a ghost for weeks.

"I'm healthy again because you've taken such good care of me. Thank you for that."

"It was my pleasure."

Hutch has been so good to me. Feeding and pampering me. Being there when I needed to talk. Or cry.

Calvin stops the car in front of my building, and I stroke my thumb over the top of Hutch's hand. I don't want him to go to work. I want him to stay with me. "You should call the office and tell them you're taking off the rest of the day."

He smiles. "That's a very good plan. So good that I'm glad I thought of it before I left the office and told my secretary that I wouldn't be returning today. Calvin, that means I won't be needing you again until the morning. I'm staying at Miss Louden's tonight."

"Will you need me to fetch Miss Ava Rose later this evening?"

Hutch looks at me for the answer. "Do you want her to come here or stay with Mrs. McVey?"

"I want her to be with us tonight." I lower my voice. "But later."

He turns back to Calvin. "We'll need you to fetch her. I'll text when we're ready for her to come."

Hutch and I were separated for more than six

weeks, but we haven't spent a night apart since we reunited. We've shared my bed for more than a month, and he hasn't tried to do anything beyond holding me against him. But that's over. My body is fully healed and we have the green light from Dr. Kimble. We both know what we're about to do.

Intimacy is our special time. It's when we come together—raw, bared, exposed. We put everything else in our world aside and make that moment about the two of us.

Once inside, Hutch wraps his arms around me from behind and holds me tightly, his nose buried in the back of my hair. "It's been so long, mo maise."

Three months feels like an eternity, especially when your separation wasn't by choice. "It's been too long since you've touched me like this."

He kisses the side of my neck, and I instantly feel those dormant tingles coming to life again. It's like a bundle of excitement stirring inside of me. "I want to take it slow and feel everything between us again."

"I want that too."

"Put on some mood music while I work on getting out of this suit. Play something soft and slow."

I made a romantic playlist before I left Hutch. I was going to play it on that last night we were together, the night our arrangement was ending, but I didn't get the chance.

I choose the shuffle option and the first song to play is "You are Mine" by MuteMath. I couldn't have picked a more fitting song if I'd gone down the list and chosen it myself.

Hutch smiles as he works on the buttons of his

shirt. "You've always known how to choose the perfect music."

Maybe it's the writer in me, but I hear a song and it always accompanies a scene playing out in my head. And I've watched the scene that goes with this song a million times.

"I want to do that for you." God, I've missed helping him undress.

I unfasten the buttons of his shirt and push it from his shoulders. I flatten my palms against his upper chest, rubbing his pecs in large circular motions, while he unfastens his belt and trousers.

Hutch has slept beside me every night for weeks. He's held me close at night, but I've resisted the urge to touch him this way, knowing what it would lead to. I held back because my body wasn't completely healed but also because my heart wasn't either. I wasn't ready.

But I am now.

He grips the hem of my dress, pulling it up and turning it into a jumble of fabric on the floor. My bra joins the growing pile of clothing, followed by my panties.

Together we move to the bed, and he lowers his body on top of me. And I realize something: home isn't four walls. It's his warm skin on my skin, his rapidly beating heart pressed against mine, and his light blue eyes locked on my hazel ones.

He kisses me softly and slowly. When he stops, his mouth is still against mine and I feel the movement of his lips. "I love you."

Warm liquid rolls away from the outer corners of my eyes into my hairline. "I love you too."

I grasp the sides of Hutch's face and kiss his

mouth. "I need us to be one. I need to feel you inside of me."

He nods. "I need that too."

Parting my legs, he nestles between them and the head of his hard cock presses against my entrance. I'm ready. He's ready. But there's suddenly an unvoiced question hanging in the air.

Birth control?

Shit.

My body has healed. I could get pregnant again if we don't use a condom, but I can't bring myself to tell him to stop. I don't want him to stop.

It may be irresponsible but he is what I need. This is what I need. And I think he needs it too.

"I don't have condoms."

"I'll pull out," he whispers against my mouth.

I kiss Hutch's mouth and lift my hips, coaxing the crown of his erection into me. It's all the invitation he needs because he pushes the remaining length inside of me until he can go no deeper.

And we are one again.

Our bodies join together and I experience peace for the first time in months. I tune out the grief and sadness and only feel the love between us. He's the calm to the storm that has been raging out of control inside of me.

I am so in love with this amazing man.

He moves in and out of me slowly, and tingly waves of sensation toss and turn deep within my pelvis. A storm of moans, groans, and panted breathing brews beneath my surface.

Bending my legs, I bring them up and wrap them around his hips. I dig my heels into his ass, making each thrust a little deeper than the one before.

His breath increases and he suddenly pulls out of me. Warm gushes of liquid splash against my stomach and oddly, I find it satisfying.

With his forehead pressed against mine, Hutch's warm breath is rapid on my mouth. I can't resist stretching up to kiss him. "I love you."

"I love you too, lass. And I'm never going to let you get away from me again."

"No worries. I'm never leaving you again."

We make up for lost time, spending the rest of the day making love. When night comes, Ava Rose sleeps between us and I feel complete. I wasn't sure that I'd ever be able to feel this way again.

But I'm afraid. There's someone out there who wants to take this happiness away from me. From us.

Please, fate. I'm happy. Don't be cruel and ruin this for me.

I want my beautiful ever after.

11

MAXWELL HUTCHESON

"Mr. Hutcheson?"

"That's me."

"Mr. Kincade will see you now."

Alex Kincade is a reputable, highly sought-after solicitor specializing in family law. Unfortunately, that means that I had to wait weeks for an appointment with him. But I'm confident that he's worth the wait. He's from Glasgow and not in the pocket of Thomas Lochridge.

"What can I do for you, Mr. Hutcheson?"

I start at the beginning and he listens intently, taking notes and occasionally asking me to clarify details about my former in-laws.

"That is one hell of a story you have there."

"Don't I know."

"How serious is your relationship with Miss Louden?"

"I'm going to marry her." If she'll have me. And if she's brave enough to take on all of the shite that comes along with being married to me.

"From what I'm able to gather, your late wife's family is going to bring Miss Louden's integrity into question. They're going to portray her as a prostitute with loose morals whom you hired for sex."

Of course, they will. Those are the kinds of bastards they are. "But that's not at all who Lou is. I'm the only client she ever had."

For fuck's sake, Lou held on to her virginity until she was twenty-two. She'd only had sex with one other man before me. She's the opposite of a whore.

Blair is married to another man and tried to suck my cock. She's attempting to blackmail me into marrying her. Her morals are the ones that should be in question.

"The sooner you're able to establish Miss Louden's character as a loyal wife and loving stepmother, the better. You should marry her quietly, as soon as possible, and work on establishing a good reputation for her through family, friends, and your staff. You'll only have until your former in-laws discover the marriage to do so."

I've been dreading this meeting because I had expected to be advised to wait on marrying Lou, not encouraged to move forward with her.

"I like your way of thinking."

"Marry your lass and sit tight. Your former in-laws will make a legal move at some point, but go about your life and enjoy your time with your new bride until they do. When it happens, all you have to do is reach out, and I'll be ready to take them on."

It feels as though a weight has been lifted from my heart and soul. I didn't realize the amount of stress I was under until some of it was relieved by this meeting with Alex Kincade.

And the plus? I get to propose to and marry Lou sooner rather than later.

Marriage isn't an in-depth conversation that we've ever had, but I know that she wants a husband and children. I just hope that she wants it with me.

A month from now is the earliest that we can be married. I need to propose as soon as possible so we can notify the registrar and fill out the appropriate forms.

All I need now is a ring and a plan.

∾

"The weather is beautiful today. Perfect for a day trip to Stirling."

A castle tour. A diamond ring in my pocket. A well-rehearsed speech in my head. But my favorite part? Lou has no idea that I'm going to propose to her when we reach the high point of the perimeter where you look out over the Trossachs.

"How in the world have you not been to see Stirling Castle?"

"My dad and Heidi didn't have interest in taking me anywhere. After I was on my own, there was no time for things like this. I had to work all of the time or the bills wouldn't get paid."

Lou's life shouldn't have been so hard. But those days are over. She's going to be mine to take care of forever.

We arrive at Stirling Castle and Lou's entire mood changes. Her eyes fill with intrigue. "Think about it, Hutch. All of the people throughout history who have traveled this stone path by foot or horse or carriage. Kings, queens, peasants. Some of them probably our ancestors."

"Aye. It's a definite possibility."

Lou stops and looks at me for a moment. "Is everything all right?"

I'm nervous as fuck and she's picking up on it. "I'm good. Why do you ask?"

"You seem distracted or something."

"It's been a long time since I've been here. I'm just taking it all in again."

Lou slips her hand in mine as we approach the entrance. "I'm sure there are at least a dozen other things you'd rather be doing today. Thank you for taking one of your days off to spend it doing something I love."

"There is nothing I'd rather be doing today more than being here with you." She doesn't know it yet but this is going to be one of the most memorable days of our life.

"Come on, Hutch. You wouldn't rather be watching rugby or football?" One of her brows lifts. "Be honest."

"I don't care what I'm doing as long as it's with you."

"That's very sweet but don't worry. We don't always have to do what I like. I'm happy to do sports stuff or whatever with you."

"I know. I'm not worried."

We go through the arched entrance and take a left into the Queen Anne Gardens. I've always thought that the area was wee and unimpressive for a castle of Stirling's size, hence the reason I'm not proposing to Lou there.

She stops and looks at everything. Every. Thing.

At this rate, the castle is going to shut down before we make it to the spot where I want to propose.

"Oh look. There's the chapel. And I hear music." She grabs my hand and tugs. "Let's go in and listen for a minute."

We work our way toward the back of the chapel and find an open area to stand and listen to the children performing orchestra music.

"That is unbelievable. I can't believe children are playing that music."

The song they're playing ends and a wee lassie, not a day over six, steps forward. A few notes fill the chapel, and I recognize the song she's going to sing.

"'Hallelujah.' I love that song."

The lyrics of the song flow from the wee girl's mouth and chills form over my entire body. She sounds like an angel from heaven.

Lou is standing in front of me and reaches for my hand, intertwining her fingers with mine, and brings our clasped hands to rest over her heart.

The song ends and Lou looks at me over her shoulder, wiping away a tear on her cheek. "That was beautiful."

"Aye, it was."

We move through the crowd and leave the chapel, continuing our tour. And finally, we approach the perimeter where you look out over the Trossachs.

"This is amazing."

"It is, but it's nothing compared to you."

A powerful gust of wind blows, and I wrap my arms around Lou from behind. I squeeze her tightly and gather my courage. And every word that I've rehearsed in my head for the last two days has vanished from my brain. I guess I'm winging this.

"Before I met you, I thought I had everything. I believed that money and success equated to happiness, but what I really had was nothing. I was empty inside, so empty that I couldn't even love the precious wee lassie that had been sent into my life. But you changed everything for me. Life as I knew it ended, and you showed me what true happiness is. You are my world, Lou. My everything. And I don't want to ever be parted from you again."

"You are my everything too. I want to be with you always."

I release my hold on Lou and reach into the pocket of my jacket, taking out the black velvet box. She turns around, I think to kiss me, and her eyes widen when she sees me drop to one knee.

"You're already mine in all ways but one. It's time to make it official. I want to give you my name. And when you're ready, I want to give you babies. As many babies as you want."

I crack open the ring box, and I can't recall ever seeing a bigger smile on her face.

"I love you, Caitriona Brooke Louden. My bonnie *Lou*. Will you marry me?"

She nods and a tear falls down one of her cheeks. "Yes. A million, billion, trillion times yes."

I slide the ring on her finger and it's a perfect fit. "Mrs. Cait Hutcheson. It sounds good but you'll always be Lou to me."

"I know. Hearing you call me Cait would just be all wrong."

I stand and she jumps into my arms, wrapping her body around mine.

"I love you." Kiss on my right cheek.

"I love you." Kiss on my left cheek.

"I love you." Long, hard kiss against my mouth.

Our foreheads are pressed together. "I'm so happy, Hutch. I can't wait to be your wife."

"If we leave now we can make it to the registrar's office before they close and notify them of our intent."

"Wow. Someone is in a hurry."

I don't want to cast a shadow on Lou's happiness, but I have to tell her what Alex Kincade has advised me to do. "I am in a hurry, and that's something that we have to talk about."

"I don't like the sound of that."

She's going to like what I have to say even less. "I had a consultation with a family law solicitor a few days ago about Ava Rose's custody. He predicts that the Lochridges will use your character as a weapon for winning custody of Ava Rose. They'll say that you're not fit to be around her because of your former employment as an escort."

"They're going to portray me as a whore."

"You and I know the truth, but it's also true that you worked at Inamorata. They'll use that information against you. Against us."

"Oh God, Hutch. I'm so sorry."

"I'm not sorry. If you hadn't taken a job with Cora, I wouldn't have met you."

"I don't want my past to be used as a means to take Ava Rose from you. I can't live with that."

"I told Mr. Kincade about my intentions to marry you. He advised me to wed you as soon as possible and to do it quietly without tipping off the Lochridges. He believes that it is in the best interest of our case to make you my wife and work on establishing a reputable name for you."

The happiness in Lou's eyes is replaced by something else. Sadness? Shame? "That makes me sound like a horrible person."

"You and I know who you are, but the Lochridges are going to make you out to be someone you're not. They will portray you to be a woman who took money in exchange for sex."

"Maybe only once and only with you, but I am a woman who took money for sex."

"They can never know about that. They'll use it against us."

"We're going to lie about our agreement?"

"If we need to." I bring her hand up and study the ring on her finger. "We love each other. You're going to be my wife. That's the only truth they need to know."

"You know they won't let that be the end of it."

Lou hasn't had an easy life. And losing our child cut her to the bone. The thought of being the person who introduces more pain and hardships into her life kills me.

"Marrying me means that there will be many difficulties introduced into your life. As much as I hate it, my problems with the Lochridges will become your problems. Being my wife won't be easy. I can promise you that much. I love you, fuck, I love you, but I understand if all of this is too much for you to take on after everything you've been through."

"I'm not afraid of difficult times. I'm pretty accustomed to them actually. And I'm not scared of the Lochridges. There's nothing they can do to keep me from becoming your wife."

"My wee fighter."

"You don't know the half of it. I retreated and let

Blair have her way because I didn't want to cause trouble for you. But that woman doesn't know me. She has no idea how hard I'll fight for those I love."

An ordinary woman wouldn't be able to withstand the shite coming our way. I wouldn't drag Lou into this fight if I thought that she couldn't handle it. But I know she can. She's the strongest woman I know. And she makes me a stronger man.

∾

IT'S OFFICIAL. OUR INTENT TO BE MARRIED NEXT MONTH has been recorded. All we have to do is plan a wedding and count down the days until Lou is my wife.

"Our wedding will need to be small without any formal announcements."

"I don't care about that stuff, Hutch. Small and hushed is fine with me. Becoming your wife is the only thing that matters to me."

Everything about this time around is different.

Mina wanted a wedding fit for a king and queen. It was a production for those within our world who Mina felt that she must impress. In the end, it was more like a runway show than nuptials.

Lou is the exact opposite. For mo maise, our wedding is about our union. Becoming husband and wife. And I adore that about her.

"I want to go to Glasgow tomorrow and tell my family about our engagement."

"I would love to do that."

And with our happy news comes sad. "I have to tell them the truth about Ava Rose."

"It's going to break their hearts."

"Aye, but I can't keep it from them any longer. The truth is going to come out eventually, and it's better if they hear it from me first."

"I know and you're right. But it's just so unfair to have your hand forced like this."

I want the entire family to be at Mum and Dad's tomorrow when we tell them about our engagement. And that means I can no longer put off telling Lou about Ian's pregnant girlfriend.

"There's something I've not told you. It's not because I was keeping it secret. I just wasn't sure how to tell you. I'm still not sure I know how."

The wind catches Lou's hair, sending it into a whirl. I wrap my arms around her and she pushes her hands into the pockets of my wool coat.

"You can tell me anything. Just say it."

It's been two months since my brother told me and the idea still hasn't sunk into my brain. "It's Ian. He's going to be a father."

It takes a moment for Lou to respond. "That's unexpected."

I know this must be painful for her to hear. "You'll be seeing the lass at my parents' house, possibly as soon as tomorrow, and she's quite pregnant."

"I didn't know Ian had a girlfriend."

"He didn't. The pregnancy is the result of a hookup, but they're exploring the possibilities of a relationship for the sake of the baby."

"What's her name?"

"Shannon. She's a nice lass. My family likes her. And my parents are excited about having another grandchild. Especially Mum."

"Do they know if it's a boy or girl?"

"A girl. Her name is going to be Pearl."

"Your first niece."

"*Our* first niece. You'll be my wife when she's born."

"That's right."

Lou is trying to be happy but I can feel her hurting. Learning about the upcoming arrival of my brother's new baby is painful for her. And I understand her ache because I feel it too.

But it won't always be like this. Our bairn will grow inside of her one day. Soon, I hope.

12

CAITRIONA LOUDEN

Calvin parks in front of Gus and Clarissa's house, and I'm anxious. My heart is pounding a million beats a minute and it has nothing to do with winning the approval of my in-laws to be. I already know that Hutch's family will be pleased about our marriage.

We should be happy about walking into this house and announcing our engagement. But instead I'm in knots because we're going to confess everything that Blair has the power to expose.

Everything about this is unfair. The way Hutch and I met is private. It should only be our business, but Blair is forcing our hand.

Bitch.

There are four cars parked in front of the house. "The whole family is here."

Great. That means that I get to confess to all of my future in-laws at the same time that I once agreed to be an escort. God, I hope they don't think poorly of me. But how could they not? Escort. The word is

synonymous with so many unsavory terms: prostitute, call girl, whore. The list goes on and on.

"Are you ready, mo maise?"

I force a smile. "As ready as I'll ever be."

Hutch leans over, cradles my face with his hands,
and kisses me. It's so soft and sweet that I feel like I'd
float away if he weren't holding on to me. "No
worries. They're going to be thrilled for us."

"I know they'll be happy about our engagement,
but it's the other stuff that is bothering me."

"It's going to be fine. Let's just get it out of the
way so we can move forward."

The scene in the Hutchesons' living room is a
surreal vision of what life with this family is going to
be like. Gus in his favorite chair. Ian sitting beside a
very pregnant woman on the sofa. Adam and the
boys sitting on the rug. Clarissa and Sara absent,
presumably in the kitchen finishing dinner.

Mason waddles over to me and reaches up,
attempting to touch Ava Rose's foot. "Bebe."

"Ah, Mason. You want to see your baby cousin?"

I bend down, bringing Ava Rose to Mason's level.
"Bebe."

"That's right. She's your baby cousin."

Mason leans forward, hugging Ava Rose, and she
squeals when he squeezes a little too hard.

"Easy, Mason. She's still a wee lassie," Hutch
says.

"Give *soft* hugs to Ava Rose," I tell him in my
"talk softly to children" voice.

Mason releases his hold and dashes back to the
rug where his toys are.

"Lou, come over and meet Shannon," Ian says.

I sit next to Ian's pregnant girlfriend and place

Ava Rose on my lap. "I'm Caitriona Louden but everyone in this family calls me Lou. And you can too."

Hutch introduced me to his family as Lou. It wouldn't feel right to tell them to call me Cait after all this time.

"It's lovely to meet you."

I might as well address the elephant in the room. The pink one. "Hutch tells me you and Ian are having a girl and her name is going to be Pearl? Is that a family name?"

"No, we just like it."

"It's a beautiful name." Very regal sounding.

"Thank you."

Shannon gestures toward Ava Rose. "Is it all right if I hold her?"

"Of course."

She takes Ava Rose from my arms and places her on her lap. "I should probably get used to this since I'll have one of my own soon."

"True. Your baby will be here before you know it."

Her pregnancy is the result of a hookup, not the coming together of two people in love. I wonder if that lessens the way she and Ian feel about the baby. Or do they already love the little girl growing inside her with all of their hearts the way that I loved my baby?

"She smells so good."

"I use lavender and chamomile baby bath-wash and lotion."

"Lavender and chamomile. I'll need to remember that."

"Ava Rose's skin is very sensitive. She has to use a

special brand and they don't sell it in the stores around here. I'll buy some for Pearl when I place our next order."

"That would be great. Thank you."

All of us move into the dining room. It's the first time all eleven—soon to be twelve—of us have come together under this roof and around this table. I'm glad everyone will be here when we share our big news. But I'm not so excited about telling them the unpleasant parts.

"The cock-a-leekie is delicious. I've never had better."

"This is my mum's version. Max has always loved it. I'm happy to teach you how to make it if you'd like."

"Yes, I would love to learn. Actually, I'd love to learn anything that you're willing to teach me about Scottish cuisine. Despite living here for so long, I still don't know how to cook many dishes."

"Don't let Lou fool you. She can cook. Cajun is her specialty."

"A Cajun meal would be a real treat. What could I do to convince you to cook for us one night?" Clarissa asks.

"No convincing needed. I'd be happy to cook for the family."

Clarissa smiles, looking at Hutch and then back to me. And then her eyes move to the enormous diamond on my left hand. "Excuse me, but do you have something that you'd like to tell us?"

Hutch reaches for my hand, cupping his around mine. "Lou and I have news to share."

All eating stops and everyone's attention focuses on us.

"I have proposed to Lou and she has agreed to become my wife. We've notified the registrar of our intent and we will be married next month."

Any doubt that I might have had about Clarissa's happiness is gone when she squeals and launches herself out of her chair, rushing toward us. "I knew it. I knew you'd be married before the end of the year. Didn't I tell you, Gus?"

"Aye. You did, love."

My mother-in-law-to-be wraps her arms around me and squeezes tightly. "I am so happy for you."

She releases me and takes my left hand, bringing it closer to her face for a better look. "A cushion-cut diamond with a pavé halo. Gorgeous. You did good, my lad."

"It's the most beautiful ring in the world." I love it.

"We're thrilled you're becoming part of our family," Clarissa says.

"I'm happy too."

This is what family is about. Happiness. Love. Affection. And I'm finally going to have that in my life for the first time.

"Congratulations. Have you chosen a date?" Sara asks.

"We're looking at the Saturday before Christmas." It's the first Saturday following the required waiting period.

"That doesn't give you long to plan a wedding. We need to go dress shopping as soon as possible. Even when you buy off the rack, alterations take time. There's really no time to waste."

"We can go tomorrow." Clarissa turns and looks

at me. "That is if you don't mind shopping for your dress in Glasgow instead of Edinburgh."

"Actually, Glasgow is preferable to Edinburgh."

Hutch looks at me and we both know that it's time. We have to tell them the rest.

"I have more news to share and unfortunately, it's not as happy."

"I'm sure it involves the Lochridges. Your bad news always does."

Gus couldn't be more right.

"Aye, and it does this time as well."

"Let me guess. They aren't pleased about your engagement?"

Oh, Clarissa. If only it were that simple.

"I'm sure they won't be pleased, but they don't yet know about our plans to marry. This is about Ava Rose."

Clarissa's eyes dart to her only granddaughter. "Is she all right?"

"She's fine. This concerns her custody."

"*Her custody?*" The muscles around Clarissa's eyes tense, deepening the lines at the corners of her eyes. "What part of her custody could possibly be up for discussion?"

"Every part of it, I'm afraid." Hutch clears his throat when his voice breaks on the final word. And my heart aches for him. This is something that he never wanted to tell his parents.

"My marriage to Mina was over long before she died. We hadn't shared a bed in over a year when she got into the car accident."

A soft gasp catches in Clarissa's throat. "No, Max."

Everyone goes silent around the table except Ava

Rose. She frets and I get up, taking her out of her high chair. And as if she feels Hutch's pain, she puts her arms out for him to take her.

"It was only natural for everyone to assume that I was Ava Rose's biological father. And I let everybody believe she was mine because I couldn't bear to add to their pain."

Clarissa's eyes glisten. "Oh, son. What a terrible burden that must have been for you to bear."

"Blair knows everything, including who Ava Rose's father is. She's using that knowledge as leverage to blackmail me."

"Blackmail you how?" Gus asks.

"She's threatening to expose Ava Rose's paternity if I don't agree to marry her."

"Marry her?" Clarissa laughs, but her laughter is clearly not induced by amusement. "I'm curious to hear how she believes you'll become her husband when she's already someone else's wife."

"She wants to divorce Doug and marry me."

"That's insane. She's aff her heid." Clarissa mutters a few more words, but I'm not able to make out what they are.

"I've met with a family law solicitor in Glasgow. Alex Kincade. I thought it would be wiser to use someone outside of Edinburgh. Someone outside of Thomas's reach."

Gus nods. "He's a wise choice. Kincade is the best in the business when it comes to family law."

Hutch reaches for my hand beneath the table. "There's more to Blair's threats and blackmail."

"Bloody hell, what else could there possibly be?"

Oh, Clarissa. There's so much more. And I hope

that you don't hate me after you find out about some of the decisions I've made.

"Blair has threatened to expose the circumstances under which Lou and I met if I don't cut all ties with her." Hutch rubs his thumb over the top of my hand. "I was very alone, and I had been for a long time before Mina died. We hadn't been husband and wife in years. I was starving for companionship."

Clarissa holds up her hand. "We're all adults here and understand what that means. You don't have to explain."

"I do have to explain because the origins of my relationship with Lou are going to come to light. Things are going to become ugly with the Lochridges, and we need you to hear the truth from us."

"We would never listen to anything the Lochridges have to say about you or Lou. The two of you are adults, and the circumstances under which you met are your business and yours alone. You don't have to tell us a thing about it."

Clarissa is giving us an out. I should be relieved and take the pass she's offering. But I can't. I'm going to be in this family for the rest of my life. I don't want the past to hang over my head.

"The truth is going to be twisted until it suits Blair's agenda. They're going to try to make me look unfit to be Ava Rose's stepmother."

I feel like I need to take this back to the circumstances that led me to Inamorata. "My father and his wife cut me off financially and made me leave their home when I was twenty-one. I got a job at a pub working as a waitress, but I could barely pay my bills. There was no way to pay for tuition with what I was earning."

I feel so much shame as I prepare to confess the rest of it. "I took a job as an escort to pay for my two final semesters at uni. It sounds horrible, I know that it does, but I only agreed to go on dates. Dinner and drinks only. No physical contact with clients."

I stop and Hutch steps in to take over the story. "The agency was having a gala to introduce new escorts to clients. I met Lou at that party and became her first client. Her first and last. And we spent the next three months together, falling in love."

Clarissa smiles. "Never be ashamed of the way you came together. Only be grateful."

Many would take this opportunity to shame me for the choices I've made, but Clarissa Hutcheson does the opposite. She's such an incredible woman. What a wonderful mother-in-law she is going to be.

"Blair has made a lot of threats but hasn't acted on any of them. We expect that to change when she finds out that Lou and I have married. Hence the reason Mr. Kincade advised us to wed quietly without calling attention to ourselves."

"Marriage isn't a secret that'll keep for long. There will be records. People talk," Gus warns.

"We know our time will be limited, but Lou is going to need people who will testify about what kind of wife and stepmother she is. We need time for her to establish that before Blair starts spewing accusations."

"I really want you to have a wedding, even if it's small and secretive. Lou has never been a bride before and she deserves that. You can't let that special day be taken away from her too."

Clarissa is so thoughtful of my feelings.

Hutch turns to look at me. "You know I'll give you any kind of wedding you want."

"I love the idea of a small, secretive wedding." It's actually perfect. I don't have anyone to invite except Rachel and Claud.

Sara pushes away from the table. "All women to the living room. Mum, grab your laptop. We have a wedding to plan and not a lot of time to do it."

Sara cracks open Clarissa's computer. "What kind of wedding do you have in mind?"

I'm not the girl who has a Pinterest board filled with wedding ideas. "I have no idea."

We've only been engaged for a day. I've barely had time for the idea to absorb into my brain.

"You should choose the venue first. Obviously somewhere away from Edinburgh so word doesn't get out."

"I love castles."

"My friend and I went to look at one a few years ago in Perthshire when she was getting married. She didn't choose it because it only accommodated twenty-four people for a ceremony, but it was breath-taking. I think it could be perfect for you and Max."

"Can you show me online?"

"Of course."

We gather behind her and look at the gallery of photographs of the castle. "Oh, Sara. That is stunning. I love it."

"You can book the entire castle and stay overnight." Sara navigates through the gallery of bedroom photos. "Look at the laird's room. Ideal for a wedding night, right?"

It's so romantic. "It's perfect."

"It even has its own wee chapel where the ceremony can take place."

"That's where I want to be married." There's no doubt in my mind.

Shannon jolts and all of our attention turns to her. "I guess Pearl likes it too. She's suddenly moving like crazy."

"I want to feel." Sara places her hand on top of Shannon's stomach and smiles. "That's one thing I miss about being pregnant. Feeling a baby move inside of you is the most extraordinary feeling there is."

I wouldn't know. I didn't get that far.

"Do you want children?" Sara asks.

"I do. Very much."

"Max has always said that he doesn't want them. That's why I was so surprised when Ava Rose came along. But I guess I know why now," Sara says.

"When we met, he was adamant about not wanting children. But something happened several weeks ago and he changed his mind."

All of Clarissa's attention focuses on me. "It must have been a big something because he has sworn for years that he'd never have children."

Do I tell them about my miscarriage or allow them to draw their own conclusions about Hutch's change of heart?

I want to tell them. I have to tell. This is my new family, and I don't want secrets between us.

"I had a miscarriage."

Clarissa leans over and wraps her arms around me. "Oh, Lou. I had no idea. I'm so sorry."

"Losing that baby changed the way Hutch felt about having children. He wants a family now."

"My heart is happy to hear that Max has changed his mind about children, but I'm also heartbroken for both of you. Gus and I lost our first bairn in my third month. That was thirty-four years ago and I still remember how much we grieved for that child."

"It's been hard. Very hard. But there was a positive to come from our loss. I have to tell myself that when I think about it or I'll start crying again."

"It's all right to cry for your angel baby whenever you need to."

Hutch has been wonderful. And so understanding. But it's nice to talk to another woman who has gone through this same tragedy.

A rainbow follows a storm, giving hope of what's to come. And I look forward to discovering my rainbow and what awaits me at the end.

13

MAXWELL HUTCHESON

"You told my family about losing the baby?"

"They asked if we had discussed children. I couldn't answer truthfully without telling them about the miscarriage. I hope you don't mind."

"I don't mind. I'm glad they know." Not telling them felt as though we were keeping a secret. And I'm so tired of secrets.

"Your mum was sad for us but also happy because you've changed your mind about wanting a family."

"Aye, she didn't miss the opportunity to corner me and put in her request for another grandchild sooner rather than later." I almost think she's afraid I'll change my mind again.

Lou giggles. "What did you tell her?"

"That we practice making a baby every chance we get."

Lou's mouth opens wide. "Hutch! You didn't."

"No, I didn't. But I would very much like to practice."

"We're in your parents' house."

She always says that. I reach for Lou and pull her against me. "We're consenting adults who are getting married in a month. I don't think they'll have an objection. And besides, Mum is the one who asked for a baby. She knows what has to be done to get one."

"True."

"You're my fiancée. Almost my wife. It isn't wrong for me to want you. And I do. I want you all the time."

Lou sits on the bed and scoots backward, spreading her knees wide. "Then I suppose it isn't wrong for you to have me."

"No. And what my mouth is about to do to you isn't wrong either."

Lying on my stomach, my face is between her thighs. Pressing my nose against her slit, I take a moment to smell her before I taste. "There's nothing in the world like your essence when you want to be fucked. I can smell your desire and how much you want it."

I allow my breath to rush over her skin, and she squirms beneath me.

"You want my tongue, don't you?"

"Yes, I want it. I always want it."

"And I always want to give it to you."

I'm dying to taste her. And when I do, she squirms her hips, grinding against my mouth, and her loud moan fills the room. Reaching up, I touch my fingertips to her lips to quieten her and she sucks my fingers into her mouth.

Fuck, it's hot. She's hot. My almost wife.

The moaning. The fast breathing. The movement

of her hips. She isn't going to last long like this. And it makes me happy that I'm able to make her orgasm so easily.

It isn't long before she tenses and quivers. And then the sweet proof of her orgasm floods my mouth. Fuck, I love the way she tastes when she comes.

She relaxes and her eyes are closed when I crawl up her body, entering her in one smooth motion while she's still savoring her post-orgasmic euphoria. I pull back and slide into her until I'm buried to the hilt again. And again.

"Ohhh." Her voice is laced so heavily with breath that the single word is almost indistinguishable. But indistinguishable or not, I understand the meaning behind it.

"Hutch." She grips my biceps and holds on when I thrust harder. "We're doing it again without a backup method."

Fuck, I don't want to use a condom. It'll ruin this for me. "I'll pull out like last time."

"We both know pulling out isn't reliable."

My head is warring with my cock. Moving inside of Lou feels so damn good and I'm close to coming. My cock doesn't give a shite about reliable birth control right now. He isn't the least bit concerned about the consequences of his actions.

"I don't have a condom." I bought some but I didn't bring them with me. I didn't know we were going to stay so late and end up spending the night here.

I move faster, bringing myself closer to orgasm. "I'll stop if you want me to." I say the words but I don't really mean them.

"God no, don't stop."

Thank fuck.

"I'll pull out before I come."

I love coming inside of Lou, but I also don't mind seeing my cum splattered across her body.

My jaw is clenched as I try to hold back and make this last for as long as possible, but I reach a point where getting off is beyond my control. "I'm almost there."

Lou cups her hands around the sides of her breasts and pushes them together. "Come between my tits."

What. The. Fuck?

Damn. Those words just did it for me.

I withdraw and she watches wide-eyed as jets of cum spurt between her tits.

We smile at each other when I'm finished and she giggles. "Well, that's a first."

It was a wee bit kinky. "What brought that on?"

"I don't know. It seemed sexy and dirty, so I wanted to see what it would feel like."

"Do you like it?"

"I don't know why but I do."

I move off Lou and lie beside her, my eyes closed, reveling in the euphoria that always follows our lovemaking. I should probably be concerned about having sex without birth control but I'm not. I'm not the least bit worried about it.

If a baby happens, it happens. Our family will grow a wee bit sooner than expected.

I reach for her hand and bring it to my mouth for a kiss. "I love you, mo maise."

She rolls from her back to her side, hitching her leg over me. Stretching her upper body across mine, we're chest to chest. "I love you too, my hot Scot almost-husband."

I stretch my neck and she does too, bringing our lips together to kiss.

"We need to have a serious conversation about sex and birth control. Initiating a discussion about it while we're in the middle of doing it isn't working."

That's probably a good idea since I lose all capacity to make sensible decisions when I'm inside of her. "Then let's talk about it."

"We were told to use a backup method during my first month on the ring and we haven't, not even once."

"That is very accurate."

"I could already be pregnant."

"I'm aware."

"We're playing a game of roulette every time we have sex, and a baby is at stake. Is that a gamble we want to continue to take or do we need to be intentional about preventing a pregnancy?"

Fate is what brought us together—twice. I think it did a good job. "I'm okay with leaving it up to fate. If a baby happens, it happens and was meant to be."

Lou cups her hand around the side of my face. "I can't believe what a different man you are from the one I met at the beginning of summer."

"I'm a different man because of you."

Lou has triggered something in me that I thought I'd never feel. All I can think about is making her mine and growing our family. "Being with you has changed everything for me. I want you to be my best friend, my wife, the mother of my children. I want you to be my number one in all things."

"I swear that I will love you beyond the final beat of my heart. And I will never hurt you."

I pull Lou close and place a kiss on the crown of her head. "I know."

Trust doesn't come easy after the things Mina did to me, but I believe Lou when she says that she'll never hurt me. I believe her when she says she'll love me forever.

Just as I will love her forever.

14

CAITRIONA LOUDEN

It's after eight o'clock when I wake and Hutch is still beside me in bed. "Good morning, mo maise."

"Good morning." I stretch and yawn, covering my mouth with my hand because I know I must have morning breath. "What are you doing still in bed?"

"I like watching you sleep. And I don't get to do it often enough because I always have to get up and get ready for work."

"You need to learn how to sleep in." I'm a pro at it. I should teach him how.

"Believe me. I'm trying."

"Leaving your position at the Lochridge firm would be helpful."

"I'll be leaving soon enough. That's why I've decided to spend what little time I have left there tying up loose ends with my clients. I don't want them to be affected because of what's happening with me."

I'm ready for Hutch to part ways with those horrid people, but at the same time I dread it because

I know all that it will encompass. It turns my stomach into a bunch of knots.

I lean over and press a kiss to the side of his mouth. "I have to get up."

He ignores my words and pulls me against him. "It's Saturday morning and we don't have Ava Rose sprawled out between us. I don't think you have to do anything but stay in this bed with me."

"I wish I could, but we're going out for breakfast and then my wedding-dress entourage and I are hitting the boutiques."

"Without Rachel?"

Is that supposed to be a serious question? Rachel would not miss this for the world. And if she couldn't make it, I'd reschedule. It's that simple.

"Of course, Rachel's coming. I texted her last night. She can't make it for breakfast, but she's meeting us at the bridal boutique."

Hutch trails his fingertips down my arm. "Ah, my bride is going wedding-dress shopping. I suppose that means I have to let you leave the bed."

"It does if you want me to have a gown to wear on our wedding day."

I'm at the mercy of in-stock dresses. We don't have time to make a special order.

"I do want to see you in a wedding dress, but I also want to see you wearing nothing on our wedding night."

"As if wearing nothing would be something new."

Hutch is so weird. I buy sexy, pretty things, and I don't get to wear them for more than two seconds before he's taking them off me.

"I happen to like it when you wear nothing."

"Oh, I know." There's zero confusion about that on my part.

"You never told me where we're getting married."

I suppose I should have consulted with Hutch about that. Oops. "A small castle in Perthshire and it is absolutely stunning. It has its own small chapel where the ceremony can take place. Looks like it would only seat around two dozen. Very intimate."

"Sounds perfect for us. What kind of dress are you looking for today?"

I wish I was one of those girls who had been looking at bridal magazines since she was twelve. Because I have no idea what I want. "I don't have any certain style in mind. I'm open to trying anything."

"I have one request I'd like you to honor."

"Anything."

"I would like it to look like a wedding dress and not like the latest trend on a fashion show runway."

I didn't expect Hutch to care one way or another about my dress. "What do you picture in your head when you imagine me walking toward you?"

"I see you wearing a long white dress and a veil. You look like a bride, not a fashionista trying to make a statement."

In other words, he doesn't want me to look like Mina. I'm okay with that.

"You want me to look like a traditional bride?"

"Exactly."

"I understand. And I have a request I'd like you to honor as well. We're getting married in a castle, and I think it's only fitting for you to wear a formal kilt outfit with the Hutcheson tartan. The sporran, the kilt hose, the flashes—all of it."

"I'd be disappointed if you didn't want me to wear it."

"Did you wear it the first time?"

"No. I wanted to but Mina thought it was too traditional and outdated. She said that it didn't complement her wedding gown."

That feels like such a missed opportunity to me. "I'm glad you didn't wear it. I want our wedding to be different."

"No worries. The most important part of our wedding is you, and you couldn't be more different. You have no idea how damn thankful I am for that."

Hutch's hand comes down and I yelp when it lands on my butt. "Get up, mo maise, and go find your dress before I give in to my urge to flip you onto your back and keep you in this bed all day."

∽

I LOOK AT DRESS NUMBER ONE IN THE MIRROR AS I STAND on the platform, and I'm immediately reminded of my first day with Cora.

I'm damaged. Something's missing inside of me. A piece of me is not here.

That's the first time I ever openly admitted that to anyone. But that part of me is no longer missing. I found it and so much more in my love for Hutch and Ava Rose.

Rachel gets up from the sofa where she and the Hutcheson women are sitting and walks closer, studying me. "I think it's beautiful, but your expression says that you think otherwise."

Rachel has the ability to read me like a book.

"Hutch wants to see me wear something traditional. I don't think a mermaid is the right silhouette."

"Too sexy?" the sales associate asks.

"I think so." I wave my hand over the top of the dress. "And I think I need more coverage in the bust area."

"No mermaids. No sweetheart necklines. That'll be helpful because it eliminates a large portion of our stock dresses."

The salesclerk returns a moment later with a few dresses draped over her arm. "These may not be what you're looking for but I want to try each one so we'll know which way to go on the silhouette."

Mermaid and trumpet? No.

A-line and modified A-line? No

Sheath? No.

Ball gown? I wouldn't have thought so but a ball gown is the only silhouette that I'll consider for our castle wedding.

The sales clerk approaches the platform with several plastic bags draped over her arm. "This will be easier now that we've narrowed down the silhouette. This one arrived a few days ago. It's a lot of dress. I've not seen it on anyone, so I don't have an opinion about it yet. Do you think it's worth trying?"

Regal. Timeless. Understated.

"I absolutely want to try on this dress."

I step into the gown and the consultant begins the daunting task of fastening the five thousand buttons up the back. "Sorry. It's going to be a minute."

"It's okay."

My back remains turned to the dressing room

mirror while she fastens the buttons. I don't want to ruin my first impression by seeing it before it's buttoned up all the way

"All done. Let's turn you around and see what you think."

Ivory. Full baroque lace overlay. Queen Anne neckline. Long sleeves.

Perfection.

I wondered how I would ever be able to choose one dress with so many to pick from but the wondering is over. When you know, you know. "This is it. This is my dress."

"You think so?"

"Oh yes. One hundred percent."

"Do you want to put on a veil so your family can get the full effect?"

"Please."

I study the image in the mirror while I wait for the consultant to return. The longer I look at myself in the dress, the more I fall in love with it.

"Here we are, dear. A tiara and veil for the princess who wears this regal gown."

She places the silver crown on top of my head, and I can't believe how much I love the way it looks with the dress.

"Do you like it?"

"I love it. It's perfect."

"I'm surprised the length is all right. I thought it would be too long, but it's perfect when you step into the heels. I don't think it'll need any alterations."

I don't point out how tall my heels are. "I think that's a good indication that this dress is the one."

"You could be right."

The consultant opens the dressing room door and I call out, "Everyone, close your eyes."

"You didn't make us close our eyes for the others," Clarissa calls back.

I take my place on the platform. "Okay. Open your eyes."

Rachel. Clarissa. Sara. Shannon. They all gasp at the same time.

"Come on, people. I need to hear your thoughts."

Rachel holds up both hands with outstretched fingers. "It's ten out of ten for me."

Clarissa nods slowly. "I love it."

"It's a stunner," Sara says.

Shannon smiles broadly. "It's fab. You look like a princess."

"It's the one, right?"

Four yeses overlap at the same time.

"This is my dress." And it's more perfect than anything that I could've hoped for.

This is what I'll be wearing on the happiest day of my life. The day that I become Mrs. Maxwell Paden Hutcheson.

15

MAXWELL HUTCHESON

Lou has been working nonstop for the last month on our wedding. Even with the help of my family and Rachel, it's still been a ton of work for her. Neither of us had any idea what it would take to pull together even a simple wedding in such a short amount of time.

We've reserved the use of the entire castle for the next three days. Everyone who will be attending our wedding tomorrow is staying at the castle tonight. And an interesting night it is going to be.

Clarissa Hutcheson has put me in the room farthest from Lou. She insists that we can't sleep together the night before our wedding or even see each other again until she enters the chapel and walks down the aisle. But it's an hour until midnight, technically not the day of the wedding yet. And I want to see my bride-to-be.

It's been a busy day. Everyone has gone to bed and the castle is finally quiet. Thank fuck. I thought they'd never settle down for the night.

I lightly knock on the door of the bride's room. A moment later she opens the door and smiles, lifting one of her brows. "What are you doing?"

"I want to see you."

Lou leans out the door and looks down the hallway. "Your mom would be livid if she knew you were here right now," she whispers.

"Why do you think I've waited until everyone has gone to bed to sneak into your room?"

"You're sneaking into my room? That sounds so naughty."

"Not near as naughty as the things I want to do to you."

"Is that supposed to convince me to let you in?"

Is she really thinking of turning me away? "Come on, Lou. I haven't been with you in days because you've been so busy with the wedding. I'm craving you."

"It's bad luck to see the bride before the wedding."

I hold up my wrist, pointing at my watch. "We have an hour until it's our wedding day, and I want to spend every minute of it with you."

She shakes her head and looks upward, murmuring something that I'm pretty sure is a profanity beginning with an F.

"Please, Lou. I'll make it worth your while."

She sighs loudly and opens the door. "Hurry up and get your ass in here before Clarissa patrols the hallway and sees you."

The door closes and I grab her around the waist, pulling her against me. "Mrs. Hutcheson."

"Not yet but almost."

"This will be our last time to fornicate."

I love the sound of her girly giggles. "I'm going to miss fornicating with you."

"You won't. Our sex life is only going to get better after we're husband and wife."

"You know what? I think so too."

I press my lips to hers and she laces her fingers through the back of my hair, pulling me closer and kissing me hard. Because we've no time to waste, I grip the hem of her nightgown and tug upward. Next goes her knickers and then my clothes.

"I don't know how many times we've done this, but I still feel flutters in my stomach every time you're this close to me. Will it always feel like this?"

"I hope so." I don't want our passion to ever fade away.

Lou's arms go around my shoulders and I grip the backs of her thighs, lifting her. She wraps her legs around my waist and I carry my almost-wife to the bed, gently lowering her to the mattress. Pushing stray hairs away from her face, I look at her eyes. "I'm so lucky to have found you."

She reaches up and caresses the side of my face. "I'm the lucky one."

When I finish kissing her, I move lower until my mouth is between her breasts. I palm one on the underside and suck her hard nipple into my mouth, swiping my tongue back and forth over it. I scrape the hard pebble with my teeth and she moans, which urges me on. And when her breath sounds like gasps, I do it again, making her breathe even harder.

I love the sexy sounds she makes when I'm teasing her. And the more I tease, the louder they become. That's something I would normally love to hear, but we must be mindful of those sleeping in the rooms next to us. "Not so loud, Lou. Someone is going to hear you."

She squirms beneath me. "How am I supposed to be quiet when you're doing all that to me?"

My mouth moves lower and hovers over her pubic arch. "Find a way, mo maise. You can do it."

I press my nose against the top of her slit. "I get to have this for the rest of my life."

"I'm glad you like it because you don't get to have any others."

"I don't want any others. Ever."

I place my fingers on the inside of her thighs and push them apart. "Do you want my mouth on you?"

Her hand rests on the top of my head, stroking my hair. "You have no idea how much I want your mouth on me."

Moving lower, I tongue her in one long, slow stroke up the center. When it hits her clit, her body jolts like she's been seared. "Like that?"

"I love it. And it doesn't matter how many times you lick me, it gets me every time when the tip of your tongue hits my clit."

I love that I'm able to do that to her. And I also love that I'm the only man who has ever put his mouth on her this way. "You always taste so damn good. I don't know if I'll ever be able to get enough of you."

"I hope you never get enough."

Her legs fall farther apart and she rocks up and down against my mouth. Pushing two fingers inside her, I use my tongue to circle that sensitive nub because I know that's what she loves.

"Uhhh… damn, Hutch."

She grips the covers on the bed with her fisted hands and her back arches off the bed.

"Uhhh… damn."

One of her feet lands on my shoulder, her toes digging into the meaty flesh, and her legs quiver on each side of my head.

"Shit… Hutch… I'm coming."

Ah, damn. She's being so fucking loud. I know someone is going to hear us.

There's no question about the moment her orgasm ends because she becomes limp as a wet noodle. She's sprawled out in her exultant state with closed eyes and a subtle smile on her face. It's satisfying to know I'm able to give her this kind of pleasure—and that she wants it from me.

Only me.

Sex is uncomplicated with Lou. No games. No tit for tat. No using it as a weapon. It simply is what it is —an honest and true physical expression of the love we share. And I'm thankful for that.

Her legs are toneless and have fallen down so I push them up, planting her soles flat on the bed. I crawl over her and lower my body to hers. "Don't you dare go to sleep on me."

"I'm not. I'm just super relaxed."

"Did you take some kind of medicine to ease the wedding jitters?"

"I don't have wedding jitters." She giggles "I'm relaxed because of that orgasm. It was amazing."

Orgasms do have a calming effect on the body. "I'm glad you enjoyed it."

I lift my head, noticing an enormous ornate

mirror propped against the wall. No doubt it's for a bride to get a full view of herself since this is the designated bride's room. But I have another full view in mind.

"Turn over."

She flips over and her eyes meet mine in the mirror. "Ohhh."

"Aye."

I lower my body and press my front to her back, watching myself kiss the side of her neck. "What do you think?"

"I've never watched myself have sex."

"Neither have I."

"Feels naughty."

"Aye, it does."

I slip my hand around her waist and lift her hips off the bed. I don't tell her so but this is something I could really get into. I'm very turned on by the idea of watching myself fuck her. It'll be like getting a glimpse of ourselves doing porn.

I grasp her hair in my fist and pull, tilting her face upward. "I want to see your face while I fuck you."

"Yes, sir."

Yes, sir? Fuck. Hearing those two words come out of her mouth while she's on her hands and knees waiting for me to fuck her feels like a whole new avenue opening up, one that needs to be explored.

Placing my cock at her wet entrance, I watch her face in the mirror, especially her eyes, as I slowly push inside of her. I never get to see her expression when I'm behind her so this is new. And it's hot.

Lou's eyes focus on mine in the mirror. "Fuck me, Hutch. You know you want to."

"Yes, I do."

After pulling back, I push into her from behind over and over. She rocks on her hands and knees, keeping perfect rhythm, meeting me thrust for thrust. And then she pushes her upper body off the bed and rises, her knees spread wide and my cock still buried inside her.

So. Fucking. Hot.

I wrap my arms around her torso and thrust upward, fucking her as she bounces up and down my cock. Leaning forward, I kiss the space between her shoulders blades as I deliver those final few thrusts. When I come, I don't pull out. I give Lou every drop that has been building inside me the last few days.

She leans back and turns her face, kissing me over her shoulder. "The next time we do this, I'll be your wife."

My wife. I can't wait for that to happen. "And I'll be your husband."

Lou relaxes and we look at our reflections. "I think we need a mirror like this in our bedroom."

"You like watching, huh?" she asks.

"I more than liked it." I think we could get very creative with it.

Pound. Pound. Pound. I'm certain before she says a word that it's my mum beating on Lou's door.

"I know you're in there, you wee jobby. I can hear what you're doing, same as everyone else in this castle. I'm giving you the courtesy of putting your clothes on before I open this door."

Lou and I laugh at the same time and my cock slides out of her. "She really doesn't want to do that."

I kiss the side of Lou's face. "I have to go but meet

me at the altar in the chapel tomorrow evening. Six o'clock sharp. Don't be late."

"I'll be the one wearing white."

"I'll be the one wearing a red and green tartan."

I yank up my trousers and toss my shirt over my shoulder. My mum is standing with her arms crossed when I open the door.

I lift my arm and point at my watch. "Well, would you look at that? Ten minutes until midnight. I'm leaving Lou's bedroom in plenty of time so I won't see my bride on the day of our wedding before she walks down the aisle to marry me. Satisfied?"

"Cutting it a wee bit close, don't you think, since you already have so much bad luck on your side? It isn't wise to tempt fate."

My mum believes in old wives' tales and the folklore that elders talk about.

"Fate didn't bring us together only to tear us apart. That's what I believe to be true."

"I hope you're right. But just in case, I have a sixpence for her to wear inside her shoe tomorrow."

All of the Hutcheson women get a sixpence coin on their wedding day. Mum sees to it. And Mina tossed the one my mum gave her into the shoebox instead of wearing it inside her shoe. She said it was ridiculous to walk down the aisle in a pair of pumps that cost a thousand pounds with a sixpence coin stuck in one of them.

"Lou will love it. Thank you very much."

Mum lifts her chin, gesturing toward the hallway. "Go on. Get in your room and let her be. Both of you need your rest for tomorrow."

"No worries. There'll be no more naughty out of

me tonight." I hug my mum and she kisses my cheek. "I love you."

"I love you too, son. And I'm so proud of the man you've become. You and Lou are going to be very happy together. This time, it's meant to be."

"Yes, it is."

16

CAITRIONA LOUDEN

I OPEN MY EYES AND LOOK AT THE TIME ON MY PHONE. It's a few minutes after seven and there's no Hutch beside me. He's up and having his first cup of tar for the day.

No, wait.

It's our wedding day.

Our. Wedding. Day.

I place my pillow over my face and squeal at the top of my lungs. I can't believe that this day has finally arrived. I'm going to become Mrs. Maxwell Paden Hutcheson this evening.

My beautiful ever after. It's mine. I'm actually getting it.

I'm changing out of my nightshirt when I hear a knock at the door. "Lou? It's Clarissa. Are you awake?"

"I am. Come in."

Clarissa has a cup of coffee in one hand and a glass of juice in the other. "I didn't think you'd be sleeping in today."

"Definitely not."

"Did you sleep at all last night or did nerves keep you awake?"

"I can't believe it, but I actually slept really well." I think that amazing orgasm was the reason.

"You're not nervous?"

I thought I would be, but I'm not. "Excited is a better way to describe how I feel."

"That's grand. You should enjoy your wedding day. Not wish it away because you're ready to put the formalities behind you."

"I have no reason to be nervous. There will only be twelve people at our wedding, and three of them are children."

"There's still time to call your family if you like. I wouldn't want you to one day regret not having them here."

Sharing DNA doesn't make them my family. "I don't want them to come."

"Are you sure?"

"They don't have a place in my life. There'll never be any regrets about them not being here."

"You are ours now, a Hutcheson, and we love you. We'll always take care of you."

I blink rapidly when I feel tears forming in my lower lids. "When you don't have a family of your own, you truly understand how important one is. And I'm so happy to be becoming a member of yours."

"I already have a daughter, but I feel like I'm gaining another one today." Clarissa looks up and touches her fingertip to the inner corners of her eyes. "That's enough of that on your wedding day. You don't want your eyes to be red and swollen, and nor do I."

I've shed too many of those salty bastards for things I have no control over. I have a wonderful life ahead of me now, and I'm done with the waterworks. "No more tears."

"The men have gone hunting. They'll be out most of the day, and Max arranged for the women to be pampered. We have a masseuse coming this morning and then a hairdresser and nail tech will be here after lunch."

That's my Hutch—always pampering me like a princess. It's what he promised right from the first and he hasn't disappointed me yet. "He loves to pamper me and I'm sure that I have you to thank for that."

"I put a lot of effort into teaching Max how to treat women well. Ian too."

"Your effort shows."

"It's taken thirty-four years, but Max is finally moving in the right direction. My worries are over with you as his wife. But Ian... I don't know about that one."

"Hutch tells me that he and Shannon are trying to build a relationship."

"Married or not, people are usually already in love when they conceive a child. I don't know how doing it in reverse is going to work for them. A bairn is very stressful. I just don't know how they can fall in love while trying to figure out how to feed and change a newborn."

"It's amazing how things can work out when you give it a shot."

"Aye. Let's cross our fingers that we'll be doing this with Ian and Shannon one day soon. Because the thought of my grandchild being raised by Shannon and a man other than Ian is more than I can stand."

This month has been dedicated to planning the wedding, so I've spent almost no time with Ian and Shannon. I have no idea what kind of relationship they have. Shannon seems nice, but I'm not really even sure what kind of person she is.

"They have all of us in their corner supporting them. Hopefully, they can make it work. And from what Hutch says, they seem willing to try."

"Aye. There's that at least."

∼

MY HOUR WITH THE MASSEUSE WAS INCREDIBLE. Exactly what I needed. I'll have to give Hutch a special thank-you for that tonight.

I'm sitting in a chair in the middle of the bride's room, and the hairstylist is curling my hair. Rachel is sitting on the bed watching her every move. "How are you wearing it today?"

"The sides will be up and the back will be down." Hutch loves my long hair when it hangs in loose curls. I wouldn't dare wear it in an updo on our wedding day.

"That'll look great with the tiara and long veil."

The hairstylist gives me a mirror when she finishes curling my hair. "Tell me what you think and if you want to change anything."

"No changes. It's exactly the way I wanted it."

Shannon comes into the bride's room and sighs when she looks at me. "So bonnie."

"Thank you."

"The photographer sent me to tell you she'll be ready for you in thirty minutes."

"It'll take that long to get you into that dress. We better get to work on those buttons," Rachel says.

I stand in my robe by the bed as Clarissa and Rachel remove my dress from the garment bag. Looking at it gives me chills.

"It's just as beautiful as I remember," Rachel says.

"Indeed, it is," Clarissa says.

It is the most beautiful wedding dress I've ever seen. The perfect shade of ivory baroque lace over creamy vanilla charmeuse—something I never imagined myself choosing. I always thought lace was old-fashioned, but this is classic and timeless. I think Hutch is going to love it.

I step into my gown and Rachel helps me pull it up. "I've been dreading these buttons since the day you bought this dress."

"I know. Me too." It's the only flaw of the dress.

"I'm going to do them up for you, lass, but it'll be Max's job to unfasten them tonight."

"He's going to be sooo happy about that." I can just see him growing impatient and threatening to rip the bodice open.

It takes a long time for Rachel to button my dress. Much longer than the consultant at the bridal shop. But in Rachel's defense, I'm sure that's something the attendant is good at because she does it on a daily basis.

"Damn, that was a lot of buttons but I'm finally done."

I walk over to the mirror and study myself. "What do you think? Anything out of place?"

"Not a single hair that I can see," Clarissa says.

Rachel assesses me. "That dress. The tiara. This castle. You look like a princess who is about to marry her prince."

My prince. My fairy tale. I'm finally getting my beautiful ever after.

It's been a long time coming. Twenty-three years in the making.

Clarissa stands behind me and my eyes meet hers in the mirror. "I get to be your mum from this day forward, and my first duty is to give you this."

I turn, looking at the coin in her hand. "Something old. Something new. Something borrowed. Something blue. And in Scotland, a sixpence in her shoe."

I forgot about that tradition. "I've been so busy planning the wedding that I didn't remember to get a sixpence."

"I'll do the honors."

I lift my dress and Clarissa lowers herself, removing my shoe and placing the coin inside. "The sixpence represents good fortune and prosperity."

"This is so thoughtful. Thank you."

I don't say so because I don't want to cast a shadow on my happy day, but Hutch and I are going to need good fortune and prosperity in our marriage with what we have ahead of us.

I wish they weren't, but Blair and the Lochridges are on my mind today. What if they've found out about the wedding? What if she shows up and tries to wreck our special day? She would have the gall to do something like that.

I'm ready to walk down that aisle. I'm ready to say I do. I'm ready to have that wedding ring on my finger. After those things are done, we'll be husband and wife, and no one can stop our marriage from happening.

I'm so close to having it all. Fate, please don't ruin it for me.

17

MAXWELL HUTCHESON

WITH THE MINISTER ON ONE SIDE AND BRADY ON THE other, I wait for my bride at the front of the chapel. It's a tiny, intimate room in the castle, barely large enough to accommodate our small wedding party.

And it's absolutely perfect.

I feel great. And happy. So fucking happy.

Lou's clever song choice, "The Secret Wedding" from *Braveheart*, begins playing, and my heart pounds because I know my bride, my secret bride, will be entering the chapel soon.

Rachel enters and walks the aisle, taking her place opposite Brady on the other side of the minister. And I'm only a heartbeat or so away from seeing Lou. And then she enters the chapel and I get my first look at my bride.

I had no idea what her dress looked like or how she would wear her hair, but everything about her is perfect. Her beauty steals the breath from my lungs, and my heart calls out to hers with an increased rhythm. My chest aches from the want, the need, the yearning to make her mine.

Our friends and family stand when they see Lou appear in the entrance of the chapel. She walks down the aisle alone, her slow steps mimicking the tempo of her favorite instrumental song, and it's the last time that she'll ever walk without me by her side.

The song fades, and the minister says a few opening words. When he finishes, Lou passes her bouquet to Rachel, and I take her hands in mine. I slowly rub my thumbs back and forth over the top of her hands as the minister begins the ceremony that will officially make this woman mine forever.

I bring her hands to my mouth, kissing both. I look at her eyes, which are more green than brown today, and I begin my vows. "Today I lay at your feet the man I have been so that I may become the man you need. I promise to be a faithful husband, a caring lover, a considerate best friend, and a loving father to our wee ones. I will always cherish and respect you, care for and protect you, comfort and encourage you, and stay with you for all eternity. I surrender my all to you today and every day hereafter."

Tears pool in her lower lids, and I catch each of them with my thumbs before they stream down her cheeks.

"Today you become my husband but also my best friend and lover. I will trust and respect you, laugh and cry with you, love you faithfully through good times and bad, no matter the size of the obstacles we face. I promise to cherish our union and every day love you more than I did the day before. I give you my hand, my heart, and my love from this day forward, for as long as we both shall live."

We exchange rings and the minister finally gets to the part I've been waiting for.

"You may kiss your bride."

I reach out, cradling Lou's face, and I kiss my wife for the first time. And it's our best kiss yet.

"I now present to you, Mr. and Mrs. Maxwell Paden Hutcheson."

~

WE SHARE A MEAL AND CAKE WITH OUR FRIENDS AND family. After they leave, we have the entire castle to ourselves. We may consummate our marriage in every room just for the fun of it. But we'll begin in the laird's room.

"It was thoughtful of your dad to come up and start a fire for us while we were having dinner."

My dad's great but he's not thoughtful. "I'm sure he was only doing what Mum told him to do."

"Either way, it's nice to have that done for us already."

"Aye."

The temperature dropped and it snowed today. The snow-covered ground made a beautiful backdrop for our wedding photos, especially the ones with the highlands in the distance.

Lou pulls her hair over her shoulder, exposing the back of her dress. "Will you unbutton me, husband?"

"I will happily unbutton you, wife."

Lou's dress is exquisite but not at all cooperative. "These buttons are very small for a man with big hands. The maker of this dress didn't have the groom or his eagerness to bed his bride in mind when he or she designed the back of this dress."

"Nor the eagerness of the bride."

That's something I love about Lou. She's always keen for sex.

My fingers brush against the bare skin on her back, and I kiss the curvature between her shoulder and neck. "Just a wee taste to hold me over."

"I wish I could help you."

"Not too much longer. I'm over halfway finished now."

I unfasten the final button, pushing the dress down her hips, and it becomes a circle of fabric that partially stands on its own. "All done with that."

Lou holds my arms, stepping out of the dress, and I suck in a breath when I see the white corset, garters, and knickers she's wearing. "I've been wondering all evening what was beneath that dress."

"And now you know."

"My wife, Mrs. Hutcheson." I've said those words before but they take on an entirely new meaning for me now. "I know you're strong and you've always taken care of yourself, but you aren't alone anymore. I'm going to take care of you, and protect you, and make sure you never want for anything in your life."

"I know you will always keep me safe. And I also know that while you talk of protecting me, you're also planning in your head how you're going to ravish me tonight."

Her comment makes me chuckle, mostly because it's true. "My wife knows me well."

I circle her, inspecting her from every angle. I wrap my arms around her from behind and my mouth hovers over her ear. "I love the way you look in this lingerie, but I want you to take it off. And I want to watch while you do it."

"Whatever you want."

I step away and watch Lou remove her corset, garters, and knickers while I shed all the layers of my formal kilt outfit.

"I'm sad to see the kilt go. I love the way it looks on you."

"Maybe I'll put it on later."

"I'd like that."

There's still a slight chill in the room so I go to the bed and remove all of the linens. I carry them to the thick plush rug in front of the fireplace and spread them out, making a place for us to lie down in front of the fire. "Is this okay with you? I thought it would be nice to take advantage of the fireplace since we don't have one in our bedroom."

"It's very okay with me."

We lower ourselves to the floor and I kneel at Lou's feet after she lies on her back. She's staring up at me, and damn, I've never seen her look more beautiful.

"I am a lucky man. If I ever forget to say it, don't think for a single second that I'm not aware."

"I'm the lucky one."

I lower myself and lie on top of Lou, pressing my forehead against hers. I close my eyes for a moment and savor the memories of this special day. Lou in her wedding gown. The vows she swore to me. The tears in her eyes and sincerity in her voice. I want to always remember the way I felt today.

"This castle has been here for more than 450 years. How many marriages do you suppose have been consummated in this room? Maybe even on another rug in front of this fireplace?"

"I don't know but one more is about to be added to the list."

I lower my lips to hers, and a soft moan finds its way from her chest to her mouth. Without breaking our kiss, I adjust my position so my lower arms on each side of her head take the brunt of my weight, and her legs move apart, allowing me to press deeper against her.

Instinct urges me to move faster. I yearn to slam my throbbing cock inside of Lou, but I make myself go slowly. Tonight is about being unhurried and making love to my wife for the first time.

I still and look at Lou's face illuminated by the flames of the fire. Warm, golden light dances upon our naked bodies as the fire crackles, and I can't think of a more perfect way to consummate our marriage.

Lowering my head, I press soft kisses against the upper swell of her breasts, first one and then the other. They're just kisses at first, until my tongue begins to lave her skin and nipples.

I've made love to Lou. I've fucked her. I've even been inside her bum. But we've never experienced this kind of intimacy. Tonight is going to mark us forever. Not only to be etched in our minds but way down into the center of our hearts where we connect —our souls. Because we belong to one another.

This woman makes me forget all of the terrible things that came before her. Only with Lou have I ever known this kind of love. And I'll never tire of the feeling.

Because this is home.

I move up again and kiss her mouth slowly. I grip her bottom lip between my teeth and tug gently.

When I do, her back arches off the floor and she presses her breasts against my chest.

Her hands move from my neck to my shoulders and down my back. Her fingers grip my arse. Our kiss deepens, and she tightens her legs around my waist.

I don't want this woman in this moment only because of how hard she makes me. I want her because of the way she softens my heart. I want her because of the way she has taught me to love.

Positioning the swollen head of my cock against her core, I enter her slowly. Husband and wife become one.

"I love you," I whisper.

"I love you too."

I move slowly, my cock sliding back and forth through her soft, slick flesh at a slow, steady pace. And I don't just feel her body squeezing mine. We connect upon a primal level, just man and woman. It's wonderful, but I know Lou's body as well as I know my own. She needs something more to bring her to orgasm. And I can't get off until she does as well.

All of my weight moves to one of my arms and I push my hand between our bodies, searching for that sensitive nub at the top of her slit. Using the pads of my fingers I pull up a little, exposing the hooded nub from its hiding place. A gasp catches in her throat and her mouth forms a perfect O, and no words are needed. I'm right where I need to be.

My cock moves in and out of her while my finger-tips rub her clit and she rocks her hips in perfect synchronization. In no time at all, her eyes close, her mouth widens, and her breathing picks up. And then

I feel those magical rhythmic contractions pulsating around my cock.

I try to hold back but my dick can't take another stroke without exploding. The climax initiates in my abdomen and pulsates into my bollocks. I'm unable to contain the groan in my chest because the pleasure of coming inside of Lou is too great.

Lou is the only woman in the world who can make me feel this way. The only one who holds my heart in her hand. The only one who wears my ring. The only one who bears my name.

My wife.

18

CAITRIONA HUTCHESON

THIS IS AN UNUSUAL MORNING. UNUSUAL FOR TWO reasons—first, I'm wearing a wedding ring on my left hand and second, I'm awake before Hutch.

I study the sleeping figure of my husband—oh damn, it's a fine one—and I can't believe it. I married the man who booked my inamorata services for the entire summer. The man who paid me to fuck him. I was his eighty-one-day whore. I can confess that sin and give it the label that it truly deserves. And I can also admit that it was the best decision of my life. Hutch is my husband—forever mine—and I couldn't be happier.

We began as strangers—as most couples do—but our beginning was very different from most. The majority would consider our introduction a perverted one. Even I did in the beginning, but then Hutch and I became so much more than either of us intended. We're Mr. and Mrs. Maxwell Hutcheson and this is the beginning of the rest of our lives.

We're venturing into the world to write our own fairy-tale love story.

I look at my husband's face and see his eyes fluttering beneath his lids. Oh, he's dreaming.

I wonder what a man like Hutch dreams about. Whatever it is, I don't want to wake him, so I slide to the edge of the bed in slow motion and place my feet on the cold floor. I look over my shoulder to make sure I haven't disturbed his sleep. He's unmoving, and I continue to ease out of the bed.

I descend the narrow, winding staircase to the kitchen on the first floor and find the breakfast pastries and fruit left for us by the staff. We opted to leave off the catering services because we wanted to be alone in the castle for the entire weekend. Hutch has to return to the firm on Monday morning and we wanted no interruptions. This is the only honeymoon we'll get for a while.

Ascending the narrow, winding staircase carrying a tray of breakfast is a little harder than it sounds. I'm winded and my muscles are burning by the time I reach the third floor where the laird's room is.

I place the tray on the table and take my time sliding back into bed. I'm so pleased with myself because I've managed to slip into bed next to Hutch without waking him. And then he suddenly rises, pinning me beneath him, a huge grin wide across his face.

"Mornin', wife." He lowers his mouth to mine and kisses me as his grin grows larger, a sweet kiss just on the surface of my lips.

"Mornin', husband."

He places his forehead against mine. "Wife. Husband. I think I like the sound of that."

"You better love the sound of it."

"Hmm. Maybe it'll grow on me with a wee bit of time."

I push against Hutch's chest and we roll so I'm on top, straddling him. I lower my mouth to his as close as possible without our lips touching. "Maybe *you'll* grow on me."

Slowly I grind against him and his hands creep up my thighs until they're on my waist. "*Something* is growing."

"That mouth of yours, Mr. Hutcheson."

"You love this mouth of mine, Mrs. Hutcheson, along with everything it does to you."

"I guess it's okay."

He grins and quickly flips us over so I'm on my back again. His mouth begins a journey at my neck and leaves a trail of wet kisses on its way down until reaching my belly button. "And this tongue of mine? Don't forget how much you love what it does to you as well."

He laves his tongue over my pubic bone and I lace my fingers through his hair before dragging my nails across his scalp. "I could never forget how talented your mouth and tongue are. Or how good they made me feel last night."

He places a kiss against my skin and looks up at me. "Our wedding night was everything you wanted it to be?"

I can't believe he thinks he has to ask. "It was perfect—everything I wanted plus a whole lot more I couldn't have possibly imagined. I didn't know I could be so happy. And I didn't know it would feel so different as husband and wife."

I beckon for him to come closer, and I cradle his

cheeks when we're eye to eye. "It was a level of inti-macy that we've never shared, and I couldn't have felt more connected to you last night. Or now."

He tucks each side of my hair behind my ears before pressing his forehead to mine. "You are my world, and I'll do anything to make you happy."

"You. That's all it takes to make me happy."

He nuzzles against my neck, and I feel the rough scruff on his chin. "This got rougher overnight."

He reaches up and strokes his chin with his hand. "Too rough for you?"

"No. I love it. It's sexy. I wouldn't mind if you grew it out a little."

"A beard?"

"I don't know. I've never seen you with a beard."

"I keep it short because it's starting to get gray in it."

I grab his face and turn it to the side for a better look. "Really?"

Hutch chuckles. "Didn't you know you just married an old man?"

I turn his face back so he's looking at me. "You're thirty-four. That's not old."

He playfully rubs his nose against mine, giving me an Eskimo kiss. "Sorry, mo maise. I got my hair from my dad's side of the family. I'm afraid that I'm destined to be an early grayer. I'll probably be more gray than dark brown by the time I'm forty."

I try to picture what Hutch will look like with gray hair, and I only see him getting better looking with age.

"So people will think you are *my* father instead of our children's father?"

"How many children are you talking about?"

Oh no. I hope he isn't rethinking his decision to have children.

My heart pounds in my chest. "I was hoping for three." I lower my voice. "Maybe four."

"In total or addition to Ava Rose?"

"In addition."

"Up to five total?"

"Yes."

Hutch chuckles. "Do you know how old I'll be when the last one is born if we wait three to four years between each bairn? Have you done the math?"

"Yes. You'll be sexy years old."

"Sexy years old. All right. I like that but, mo maise, I'll be approaching fifty."

"Then maybe we have them two years apart instead of three or four. You'll still be early forties when the last one comes."

"And you'll be thirty-ish with five wee Hutch-esons." He moves over my face and his voice is breathy against my ear. "You've turned my world on its head, making me change everything I thought I wanted for my life. You know that, right?"

"I do and it doesn't go unnoticed." And to know that I hold that kind of power over him shows me how much he adores me.

He runs his nose down the length of my neck, and his breath is warm on my skin. He knows how much that turns me on. "Maybe we should practice making babies so we'll be really good at it when the time is right for trying."

This beautiful man wants to create life with me. Another little life.

"I've heard it said that practice makes perfect."

"That's right."

He kisses my mouth so lovingly. It isn't urgent like so many of our kisses are. It's sweet, and he makes me feel so loved.

And breakfast is forgotten. At least for now.

19

MAXWELL HUTCHESON

"WELL, I'LL BE DAMNED," BRADY SAYS, STANDING IN the doorway of my office. "You said you'd be here today, but I didn't believe you actually would be."

This morning was a strange one. Lou and I got up and returned to our lives as though we didn't get married on Saturday and spend the rest of the weekend in each other's arms as newlyweds.

Damn. Walking away from her this morning was so much harder than I thought it would be.

"I'm not here because this is where I want to be. That's for damn sure."

Lou and I have a difficult task ahead of us, and we can't afford to call attention to ourselves. As much as I despise it, I have to play the dutiful Lochridge Investments employee for a little longer in order to buy the precious time we need to build Lou's character.

I beckon Brady to come into my office. Too many ears around this place. "Shut the door."

"I assume you enjoyed the weekend with your bride?"

"Definitely not the honeymoon I would have chosen to give Lou but it was still grand. We enjoyed our time at the castle."

"I know it's very early on but how does marriage feel with a different woman?"

"It's amazing this time. So very different than before." I never doubted that it would be.

"No regrets?"

"Not one."

"I don't think I'll ever marry again."

Brady is afraid of getting it wrong a second time. And I understand that feeling all too well.

"I think you'll feel differently when you meet the right woman."

"I don't know, mate. I think I could be fucked up in the head where women are concerned."

"I don't know the answer. I only know that I almost lost Lou because I wasn't receptive to falling in love with her. My advice is to keep an open mind."

"It's been a long time since I was with a woman who wasn't paid to be with me."

I'm surprised Brady hasn't grown tired of inamoratas. He was once a faithful, loyal husband. "If you're content, then continue doing what you're doing. If there comes a time when you're no longer happy with inamoratas, do something else."

Brady rubs his palms over his face. "I don't know what's wrong with me. I'm suddenly questioning my life and what the fuck I'm doing with it."

"I think we all do that from time to time."

"I was fine until I saw how happy you were with

Lou, and I became restless. If I'm being honest with you about it, I envy what you have with her." Brady chuckles. "Fuck, I sound like a pussy talking this way."

"Maybe you should talk to Cora about finding a long-term inamorata for you. Someone like Lou who will give you the full girlfriend experience."

"That's not the worst idea you've ever had."

"Who knows? You could find the one just like I did."

My phone rings and I pick up the handset. "Yes, Mary?"

"I'm sorry to bother you but you have a visitor. Miss Blair is here and wants to see you."

Motherfucker.

I haven't seen Blair since she gave me the marriage ultimatum. I've been avoiding her like the plague she is. And now she's here at the firm, making it impossible for me to evade her. She's cornered me inside of her father's lair.

But I've had time to plan out how I'll handle this with her, and I'm prepared. "You can send her in."

I lower the handset to its base.

"Client?" Brady asks.

"No, it's Blair."

"Do you know what you're going to say?"

"I have a plan but who knows how she'll respond. This all goes to shite if she doesn't go along with it."

The door opens and Blair smiles when her eyes meet mine. And then she notices Brady. "Mary didn't tell me you were with someone. I hope I'm not interrupting business."

It would be the first time she didn't want to interrupt.

"No interruption. Our meeting was over so I was just leaving." Brady nods at Blair. "Lovely to see you, as always."

"And you as well," Blair says.

Brady stops in the doorway and turns around. "You've not forgotten our twelve o'clock lunch meeting with Gillespie?"

Brady is a fast-thinking son of a bitch, and I'm proud to call him my best mate.

"Aye, I haven't forgotten."

"We need to leave in about fifteen minutes if we're going to make our reservation on time."

Thank you, mate. I owe you a big one.

"I'll be a few minutes with Blair, and then I'll swing by your office."

"Grand."

Brady leaves the door open on his way out, I'm sure to annoy Blair. He hates her as much as I do, but this latest stunt of hers has deepened his hatred.

She goes to the door and closes it. "I guess we don't have long to talk."

"We don't."

"I came to your house every day this weekend and you were gone. Where were you?"

Fuck. I hate the way she presumes to have the right to question me about my whereabouts. She's like Mina in so many ways.

"My family took a weekend holiday."

"Special occasion?"

"We haven't been on holiday as a family in a while and Mum wanted to spend the weekend together."

"So close to Christmas?"

"The timeline wouldn't allow us to wait."

"What timeline is that?"

"Ian is going to be a father soon. The bairn is scheduled to arrive next month. Mum wanted to do it before the baby comes."

"Isn't Ian still at uni?"

"Aye, he is. One more semester to go. He'll graduate in May."

Blair looks as though she's smelling something putrid. "Your parents must be humiliated."

"They weren't ecstatic about it at first, but they've come to accept it. And they're happy about getting another granddaughter."

Blair laughs and shakes her head. "You've been a part of our family for so long that I sometimes forget what kind of people you really come from."

I would ask her what the fuck that means except that I already know it's an insult targeted at my family. Mina did the same thing, often jabbing me with insults about my family not being from the same stock as hers.

"I don't think you came here to talk about my family holiday."

"You know why I've come. You've had plenty of time to think about my proposition. What is your decision?"

I don't like this. I don't like pacifying her. I don't like not telling her to go fuck herself.

"There are a lot of holes in your plan."

"Such as?"

"You're married."

"And I told you that I would divorce Doug and marry you."

"An uncontested divorce takes two to three months, but your divorce won't be a simplified one.

Doug will contest it, and it'll drag on for at least a year. Possibly longer considering the involvement of your monies and property."

It's a legitimate argument. Even if Doug doesn't love Blair, he won't agree to walk away with nothing. Only a fool would do that.

"Doug won't contest. Dad will ensure that."

"Have you discussed this with Thomas?"

"No, but he'll go along with it. He's never liked Doug anyway."

"Have you considered what people will say about us being together?"

"They'll eventually accept us as a couple. It won't be a problem."

Buy time with her, Max. That's all you have to do right now. Even if you want to chew off your tongue in the process.

"I love my daughter and I don't want to lose her. If I have to marry you to keep her, then I'll do it."

"Well, it's not the proposal I was hoping for, but I guess it'll have to do."

Sorry, bitch. You don't get a romantic proposal when you're trying to blackmail someone into marriage.

She comes to me, wrapping her arms around my shoulder. I grip her wrists, lowering them to her sides. "There'll be none of that."

"There'll be none of what?" She may be asking but she knows exactly what I mean.

"No touching. No kissing."

"You're going to be my husband, and this is going to be a real marriage. Intimacy and sex will be part of that."

The thought of fucking Blair nauseates me.

"Maybe so but I can't be with you while you're married to another man. Mina betrayed me that way, and I can't be a part of doing that to Doug."

My brother-in-law doesn't understand the favor I'm doing him by convincing Blair to file for divorce. He's probably been wanting out for years.

"Doug doesn't deserve to be betrayed because you've decided that you don't want to be married to him anymore."

"It sounds as though you care more about Doug than about me."

Doug has been my brother-in-law for years. We've never been extremely close, but I still consider him family. And I don't have to care about him a lot in order to care more about him than I do Blair.

Come on, Max. Tell her what she wants to hear and make her happy. Her contentment is what buys you time. "How soon can you file for divorce?"

"I'll call today for an appointment with a solicitor."

"Today is good. The sooner, the better."

"I like your eagerness."

She won't like what I have to say next. "We can't spend time together while you're still married."

"What? Why?"

"Judges frown upon adultery in divorce cases. We can't give anyone grounds to suspect anything between us." And I need a reason to not spend time with her.

"That could be a year away. I'm not waiting that long to be with you."

"This is a pivotal moment. What if Doug hired a private investigator and he took photographs of us together? He could use that against you in court. And even if it didn't help his case, the truth about us would be out there. I wouldn't want anyone to think I was having an affair with you prior to Mina's death. And that's how it would look to people if we're together before you're divorced."

"I guess you're right. I'm being impatient."

I bring my arm up, looking at my watch. "I have to go. Brady will be waiting for me."

"When can I see you again?"

Never again would be too soon.

"Get the divorce in motion and we'll talk in a month."

"I don't want to go a month without seeing you."

"If this is what you want, then this is the way it has to be. And there'll be no more discussion about it."

Blair grins... and looks as though she wants to fuck me more now than she did the night she was on her knees trying to unbuckle my trousers.

"*Yes, sir.* If that's the way you want it."

Yes, sir? What is happening here?

Does she like it when I take control? Does she like being told what to do?

Maybe. It's something that could be worth exploring in the future if need be.

"Will you come to Mum and Dad's for Christmas?"

"I'm spending Christmas with my family."

"What about Ava Rose? She should be with us during the holidays."

"I'll call Lundy and make arrangements for her to spend time with your family."

"We won't have this problem after we're married. She'll be our daughter and we'll raise her together."

Bairns. I've never heard Blair say if she wants her own or not. As far as she knows, I can't father children. That might be a good angle to work.

"If you want to have children of your own, I won't be able to give them to you. I'm sterile."

I laugh a wee bit on the inside as I say the words. I'm pretty sure I'm the opposite of sterile since Lou became pregnant while she was taking the pill.

"Mina was always a failure. I won't be. I'll have your babies."

"*I* was the problem. Not Mina."

"Then we'll do in vitro."

"That's not guaranteed to work. Do you really want to enter into a marriage with a man who can't give you children the natural way?"

"You know I always get what I want and I want children. I'll find a way to make it happen."

Sorry, Blair. I wouldn't be able to get my cock up for you if you were the last woman on earth.

"I have to go. Can't keep this client waiting."

20

CAITRIONA HUTCHESON

"MUH... MUH... MUH." I WAKE TO A SOFT PALM patting the side of my face, and my heart melts when I hear what I think is Ava Rose trying to call me mum. Maybe.

Hutch insists on teaching her to call me mum because he says that I'm the only mother she'll ever know. In our situation, I'm not sure it's the best idea, but it's what he wants. And I certainly don't mind. No matter what happens, I will always consider her my child.

Gripping her wrist, I bring her palm to my mouth and kiss it. "Good morning, baby girl."

"I tried to convince her to sleep a little longer but she's not having it. It's as though she somehow knows it's Christmas morning, and she has gifts under the tree."

My little brother and sisters always somehow knew too. Weird how that happens with kids.

"I say we let her tear into them."

The three of us move into the living room and sit

on the floor by the tree. Hutch places a gift in front of Ava Rose. "Go for it, lassie. Tear the paper."

I reach over and rip it a little, widening my eyes and mouth when it makes a tearing sound. "See? It's okay to tear it."

She pulls and giggles when the paper tears. Baby giggles. They're the absolute best thing in this world.

"I think you're going to need some help or this will take all day, little lady." And we don't have all day. We have to be at Gus and Clarissa's at twelve.

This. This is everything that I imagined in my head when I dreamed about Christmas morning with my someday family: a handsome husband who loves me. A child who adores me. A happy home filled with love and laughter. This is my beautiful ever after. It's mine. It's actually mine.

Hutch stretches and grabs one of the gifts, placing it on my lap. "From Ava Rose and me."

"She helped you pick it out?"

"She absolutely did."

I lean down and tell her, "Then I know it's the best gift ever."

I tear the paper away and squeal when I see the white box and Apple emblem. "Oh my God. A new laptop?" And not just any ole cheap laptop. It's the best one on the market.

"You don't have to worry about this one crashing."

This computer will do everything I need it to do. "I needed this so much. Thank you."

"I kept thinking you would buy one for yourself, but you never did."

So much has been going on. "Our lives have been so busy. Something kept getting in the way."

"Everything from your old laptop has been transferred to this one. You're all set to write a bestseller."

I might have once thought of this as a "too-practical present" but not today. This gift shows me how well Hutch knows me. How much he loves me. "I love it. This is great. Such a thoughtful gift. Thank you."

"I hope you're able to use it to make your dreams a reality."

I'm the wife of a man who makes a shit ton of money. We certainly don't need the funds that would come from the sales of a bestseller, but he never discourages me from finishing uni or chasing my dream. He wants me to be a successful writer, but mostly he wants me to do what makes me happy and I love him for that.

"Thank you for encouraging me."

"I always want you to live your best life, mo maise."

"I know you do." And there is no life better than this life with him and Ava Rose.

"We have another gift for you, and I'm certain that you're going to love it even more than this one."

"I don't know how it could be better than this one." I hold up my laptop. "This is pretty freaking awesome."

"I've been dying to tell you about this. I was so close to blurting it out. In fact, I almost let it slip a time or two."

What in the world could it be? "You're killing me, Hutch."

He places another gift in front of me and I tear into it, filled with excitement like a child. Because I sort of do feel like a child. I didn't grow up having

Christmas mornings like this. But I keep that to myself. I don't want to put a damper on the happy time we're having.

I lift the top of the box and inside are several pieces of baby-pink fabric. And I'm confused. "I don't... these are very pretty, but I don't know what they are."

"I'm going to have Ava Rose's nursery moved to the room across the hall from our bedroom. These are some swatches that the interior designer sent over for you to look at. You get to choose the colors, the design, the theme, everything."

"Aww, Hutch." I clutch the fabric against my chest. "This makes me so happy."

"I thought it might."

"Are you doing this because you want her back in her bed instead of ours?"

"I love her, but she's hell to sleep with."

Ava Rose squirms until she wedges herself sideways between us. Her feet always end up on Hutch and he takes a good kick to the face almost every night.

"I know you're the one who takes the brunt of it every night. I understand. And I can live with her being across the hallway."

Out of sight, out of mind. That was the idea behind the placement of Ava Rose's nursery a year ago, but so much has changed since then. This little girl isn't meant to be unseen and unheard.

She is meant to be held, kissed, and loved. She is meant to be held, kissed, and loved *by me*. I am her mother. And I couldn't ask for a better gift than that.

"I have a gift for you too."

"The enormous one that somehow magically appeared behind the tree since last night?"

"Yeah. But you've got to help with it. It's heavy."

"What in the world is this?"

"Tear off the paper and see."

When the paper is gone he looks at the six-foot mirror—which I plan to prop against the wall in our bedroom—and he grins. He grins big. "Please tell me you bought this so we can relive our time at the castle."

"Yesss. You remember."

"I may forget a lot of things but what we did in front of that mirror will never be forgotten."

"You like it?"

"I love it. Best wife ever." He reaches out and grabs me by the waist. Pulling me into his arms, he kisses my face and the side of my neck. "Grrr... I fucking love it and I can't wait to try it out."

"Me too."

I turn in his arms and together we watch Ava Rose playing with one of her new toys. "This is the best Christmas morning I've ever had. I don't want it to end."

"It's the best one I've ever had too. And we have all morning to enjoy it," he says.

"I've never been happier."

"This is only the beginning of our happy life together, mo maise. We have so much more happiness ahead of us."

"I know. And I look forward to spending every day of my life with you and Ava Rose."

Hutch squeezes me in his arms and kisses the top of my head.

"I was thinking about cooking breakfast. Maybe

some biscuits and gravy? We haven't had that in a while."

He moans against my ear. "Mmm… that sounds good."

"Just biscuits and gravy or do you want bacon and scrambled eggs too?"

"I want it all."

I don't know what I was thinking. He always wants it all.

"Do you want your coffee now?"

The doorbell rings and I turn in his arms to look at him. "Are you expecting someone?" he asks.

"No." Who the hell would I be expecting?

"It's probably Mrs. McVey coming to see Ava Rose," he says.

Mrs. McVey loves our girl as much as we do. There's no doubt about that. "I bet you're right. Go let her in before the poor thing freezes out there."

Ava Rose frowns when Hutch leaves the room and crawls to me, holding up her arms. "Muh… muh."

"It's okay. Daddy is coming right back."

She's been going through a phase lately. We can't walk out of the room without her fretting. One of us has to be in her sight at all times. Separation anxiety, I guess, but I don't mind. I love that she feels safer when she's with us.

"What are you doing here?" Hutch's voice carries into the living room, and his tone tells me that he's not happy.

Shit. That is not Mrs. McVey at the door.

21

MAXWELL HUTCHESON

MOTHER. FUCKER.

"What are you doing here?"

"What do you mean what am I doing here? It's Christmas morning. I want to see my fiancé, of course."

"I told you I was spending Christmas with my family." And I bought myself a month of Blair-free time. Or so I thought.

"But you aren't going to Clarissa and Gus's until later so your morning is free, right?"

"I'm spending the morning with my daughter." And my wife.

"She's my niece, and she's going to be my daughter soon. I should spend Christmas morning with her too."

"No." I'm taking a chance by rejecting her but I don't care. I won't let her ruin this day for us.

"What do you mean no?"

"This is our special time."

"You don't want me here?"

How can she possibly think I would? "No, I don't."

"Is someone here?"

I say nothing, contemplating the shite storm that would erupt if I told her the truth.

Lou has been back in my life for two months. Two months is a long time for pretending. Living a lie is exhausting and I'm tired of it.

Blair pushes past me and I follow her to the living room. I'm ready for this. I'm prepared for the fight that is about to happen.

"Muh… muh… muh." Ava Rose is crawling across the living room floor toward the hallway leading to our bedroom. Calling out for her mum. Lou.

Where did Lou go?

"There's my lassie," Blair says as she goes to Ava Rose, picking her up. "How are you, my angel?"

Ava Rose looks at Blair, her bottom lip quivering, and bursts into a full-on tantrum. And I don't blame her. I have similar feelings when it comes to Blair.

I hold out my arms. "Give her to me."

Blair turns, holding my child out of my reach. "She just needs to get used to me."

Ava Rose screams and reaches for me. "Da. Da. Da."

"You're scaring her. Give her to me."

Blair ignores my demands, bouncing Ava Rose up and down on her hip, and the urge to place my hand around the bitch's throat grows stronger as my daughter's screams become louder.

"I'm not fucking with you. Give her to me. NOW!"

Blair's eyes widen and she turns, holding out Ava Rose. "Fine. Take her."

I cradle her in my arms and she tightly clings to my shirt. "Don't ever do that to her again."

"She'll get used to me if you'll stop coddling her."

I don't want Ava Rose to ever spend enough time with Blair to get used to her. "She's a bairn. She needs coddling to feel safe. And you're the last person on earth who needs to tell me how to care for my daughter."

Blair sighs. "Will you please just let the nanny take her so you and I can have a pleasant Christmas morning?"

"Mrs. McVey isn't here and even if she was, I wouldn't ask her to take Ava Rose. I want to be with my daughter."

Ava Rose looks over her shoulder at Blair. As if someone cues her, she vomits and the spit-up splatters on Blair's shoes and pants when it hits the floor. I couldn't have orchestrated it better if I'd tried.

"Fuck," she yells. "These shoes are brand new."

Ava Rose jolts in my arms and begins to sob loudly when Blair raises her voice. "I want you to leave."

"Come on, Max. She's a baby. Babies cry."

"She wasn't crying before you got here. In fact, she was quite happy. We both were."

"That's a rude thing to say to me."

"Well, you should easily recognize rude when you hear it since it's a language you speak fluently."

Blair holds up her palms. "Both of you are clearly having a bad morning. I'm going."

Thank fuck.

"I'll see you tonight when you bring her to Mum and Dad's."

I hug Ava Rose and kiss her forehead, swaying back and forth. "I'm so sorry for that, baby. Da is so sorry."

I hear the front door open and close and I call out to Lou. "She's gone."

Lou comes to us and takes Ava Rose from me. "Do you have any idea how difficult it was to not come out here and kill her?"

"I have a pretty good idea."

"I understand we're doing this because it's what your legal counsel told us to do, but everything about this feels wrong."

"I know, and I couldn't agree more."

"What do we do from here? Because I can't let her do that to Ava Rose again."

"I don't know. Let's just get through the holidays, and we'll figure out something after the new year comes."

"If I can make it that long without killing her."

"Speaking of the new year. We've been invited to a New Year's party."

"*We've* been invited? As in you *and me*?"

"Well, technically, I was the one invited but only because they don't know you're my wife."

"I assume you're telling me about this party because you want to go?"

"I'd like to. I think it would be fun. And you'd get to meet some more of my friends and their wives."

"How are they going to feel about you showing up with a new wife they know nothing about?"

"No worries. It'll be fine."

"You don't think anyone at this party will expose us?"

"Trust me. There won't be any problems with these people."

"Okay. That's all you have to tell me about it."

I pick up Ava Rose's hand and use it to pat Lou on the shoulder. "Mum mum," I whisper in my best baby voice.

"Yes, baby Ava?"

"Da is hungry."

"He still wants breakfast?"

"Yes."

"I'll cook for Da under one condition. He has to clean up the puke on the floor."

Dammit. I knew that was coming.

I groan. "I must really want your biscuits and gravy to agree to that."

"Well, somebody's gotta do it."

"Aye, the one who should have to do it is gone."

Lou kisses the top of Ava Rose's head. "And thank God for that."

"I'll clean up in here and then I'll come feed her while you cook breakfast."

"Deal."

We make a great team.

22

CAITRIONA HUTCHESON

"ARE YOU SURE IT'S OKAY FOR ME TO GO TO THIS PARTY with you?" It feels extremely risky to expose ourselves to clients who have contact with Thomas Lochridge.

"The Breckenridges aren't typical Lochridge clientele. They're my friends and they want to meet my wife."

"You told them we were married?"

"Aye, I did when I accepted the invitation. I also made them aware of our need to keep our marriage secret."

"They must be very close friends for you to confide in them something so important."

"The Breckenridges are loyal people. They'd never betray my confidence, same as I would never betray theirs. Believe me when I tell you that no one understands the importance of concealment more than they do."

"That's an odd thing to say about friends."

"They are my friends and that means they will be

your friends. But never ask me or them about their secrets. It isn't safe to be privy to their private matters."

I know Hutch deals with clients who have questionable backgrounds, but I've never dreamed that any of them might be unsafe. "Are you in danger?"

"Not today and not in the foreseeable future."

That's not a no. "Nothing about that statement is reassuring."

"I'm safe, mo maise. Nothing is going to happen to me, and that's all you need to know."

"Is Brady friends with the Breckenridges?"

"He is, but he won't be there tonight. He's closing on an arrangement with Cora for a three-month companion."

"I didn't take Brady for the long-term kind of client." He seemed to be happy having a different girl every time.

"He was content until he saw how happy we are."

"And now he wants what we have?"

"Everyone wants what we have." Hutch grins. "Minus the pain-in-the-arse former in-laws."

"I guess it makes sense that he would let Cora do his matchmaking. She's been choosing his inamoratas for him for years."

"She knows his preferences well."

Cora is good at what she does, which is why it was important that she knew about the behavior of her son. I told her about his attack on me, not to mention releasing Inamorata information to Blair. In Cora's line of business discretion is her highest priority.

"I wonder if I know her—Brady's match."

"I don't think you do. She's new. Never had a client before."

New inamorata. No former clients. Three-month arrangement. "That sounds familiar."

"Very familiar. And I'm hopeful for him. He'll make a good husband for some lucky lass."

It worked for us so who's to say that Brady didn't just meet his future wife.

Speaking of wives. "Who will I be meeting tonight?"

"Oh, let's see. Sin and Bleu. Mitch and Shaw. Jamie and Ellison. Kieran and Westlyn. Leith and Lorna."

Ten of Hutch's friends all at once. That's a little daunting.

Cora taught me how to converse with the wealthiest and most influential men in Scotland, but this feels different. "I'm nervous about meeting them."

"Why would you be nervous?"

Hutch and I live in a bubble. Aside from his family and Brady and staff, I don't know the people in his life. "I'm your wife, but I'm nothing like the people you associate with on a daily basis within your *Maxwell Hutcheson* world."

"And thank fuck for that. I would never want you to be like the people in my *Maxwell Hutcheson* world. I want you to be like the people in my *Hutch* world."

"I want to be myself with your friends, not speak or act the way Cora taught me. But I also don't want to embarrass you by being simple." I have the ability to give the performance of a lifetime. I was taught by the best, but I don't want to be fake if these people are going to be my real friends.

"Mo maise—" Hutch takes my hands in his. "Being unpretentious doesn't make you simple. It makes you real and genuine. That's all I ever want you to be."

Doubt creeps into my mind. I will it to go away, but it's a part of me deep as my soul. "What if they don't like the real me?"

"That's not even a possibility. You're the most lovable person I know."

I'm his wife. He has to say that. "I'm the most lovable person to you. Everyone else in the world doesn't feel that way."

"I think you will get on quite well with all of the wives, especially Bleu and Ellison. They're American."

I wasn't expecting that. "From where?"

"I don't recall, but they do have accents similar to yours."

Southern girls? You don't run into those in Edinburgh every day. "Have they lived here for long?"

"Several years. I'm not certain how long."

My mood just shifted from worried to enthusiastic. I suddenly don't feel as though I'll be quite so out of place with these people. But I'm a little confused by their dynamics. "A pair of sisters married a pair of brothers?"

"No. Bleu's husband, Sin, and Ellison's husband, Jamie, are cousins. Mitch and Sin are brothers. Kieran and Shaw are brother and sister. Jamie and Westlyn are brother and sister."

Wow. That's not confusing at all. "They believe in keeping it in the family, don't they?"

"No doubt about it. The Breckenridges keep the family tree well pruned."

"Their family... is that like a modern-day clan thing?"

Hutch chuckles. "That wouldn't be an entirely wrong way of looking at it."

He's being vague. I assume that means I should stop asking questions.

I stand tall and smooth the front of my dress. "Do I look all right?"

"Stunning as always."

"Complimentary as always."

"A husband should tell his wife how beautiful she is and often."

"You certainly do that."

My past has made me quite the cynic. It hasn't been easy but I'm in a place where I'm finally able to accept Hutch's compliments. I believe him when he says I'm beautiful because I know that's how he sees me.

I'M NOT SURE WHAT'S GOING ON WITH THESE TEN people. I have no idea what kind of secrets they're keeping, and according to Hutch, I never will. I also don't know why there would be danger associated with them. I have a few guesses, but there can only be one at the top of my list. And if I'm right, it scares me to death to think that my husband is part of their world.

The only thing I know for sure is that I like these people, dangerous or not.

"I haven't heard a N'awlins accent in years," Ellison says.

"I've been gone from New Orleans for seven

years. People tell me I still have the accent, but I don't hear it."

"Oh, darlin', you might not have it like you did seven years ago, but it's definitely there. Just like Bleu and I still have our Southern accents. It's impossible to shake that shit completely."

Ellison is so frank. And funny. I wasn't expecting the wives of Hutch's friends to be so personable.

I love Rachel and she will forever be my best friend, but she doesn't have a lot of time for me these days. And that's fine. She needs to work on her relationship with Claud. And I need this. I need friends in my life. And I think I just found five new ones.

"I want to ask you guys something."

Sure, okay, and aye all overlap at once.

I can't believe I'm going to do this. "You knew Mina?"

"Not well but we were acquainted," Bleu says.

Damn. They're probably going to think I sound jealous of a dead woman when I ask this. "I only know what Hutch has told me. What did you think of her?"

"We can talk about Mina, but first can I just say that I think it's the cutest thing ever that you have given Max the nickname Hutch? And I love that he calls you Lou. It's so adorable."

"Ah, thanks. He's been Hutch to me since the night we met. It feels odd when I hear people call him Max, but Maxwell is even weirder to me. It's so stiff and formal and I don't see him that way at all."

"Well, darlin', I hope you see him stiff sometimes." Ellison shrugs her shoulders when she looks at her sister. "I'm sorry. I had to. She walked right into it."

Bleu rolls her eyes. "Please allow me to apologize for my sister. She can be highly inappropriate at times."

"It's fine. I appreciate witty banter." I haven't laughed this much in… ever. It's nice.

I wish Hutch and I laughed more often. But how can we when the burden of the situation ahead of us weighs so heavily on our minds?

"You want to know about Mina? I'll tell you all about Mina. She was a rude bitch," Lorna says.

Wow. I'm loving the brutal honesty coming from these ladies.

"Lolo, you know it's wrong to speak ill of the dead," Westlyn says and then turns to look at me. "But she's right. That woman was a very rude bitch."

Lorna continues, "She had a way of looking at you as though you were no better than the dirt beneath her designer pumps. You know the look I'm talking about?"

I know it well. "Must be a Lochridge trait because her sister looks at me just like that."

"You have no idea how many times I wanted to say 'Bitch, I'm married to a Breckenridge. You have no idea what I could have done to you.'"

Ellison's statement carries a lot of weight. Normal, everyday people don't make threats like that. Sure, we say that we're going to jack someone up or slap them silly but not that we could have things done to people. Those are a very telling choice of words.

Bleu looks at her sister, her brow lifted. "Elli—" There's a warning tone in her voice. It's unmistakable.

"Sorry, Cait. I get a little fired up about shit like that and spout off at the mouth."

"I understand. If Mina was anything like her sister, she'd be enough to make anyone get fired up. She won't leave us alone. And she's threatening to take Hutch's daughter from us."

Westlyn reaches over and places her hand on mine. "I'm sorry she's giving you problems. There must be some way to put a stop to that nonsense."

"Hutch has seen a family law solicitor. His advice was to establish my character as a loving wife and stepmother to Ava Rose. We'll need character witnesses when we go to court."

Ellison throws her hand up, waving it back and forth. "Oh no, sweetie. You need to put a stop to that shit before it ever goes to court."

"I would love nothing better but the Lochridges are powerful. I'm not."

"Powerful people always have weaknesses and secrets. Usually big ones. You just have to find them," Bleu says.

"I wouldn't know where to begin."

"It's as simple as pen and paper. Start making lists of what you know to be facts about Mina and her family. Make another list of things you suspect. You'd be surprised by how the two lists will coincide and bring the pieces of the puzzles together." Bleu weaves her fingers together, forming a clasp. "Each piece will build upon the next."

"You should listen to her. She knows what she's talking about. She used to be an FBI agent," Westlyn says.

"FBI? Federal Bureau of Investigation? That kind of agent?"

"Yeah. Badge-wearing, gun-carrying certified badass in blue," Ellison says.

I guess I'm being sexist in my own head, but I would have pegged her for a model before an FBI agent. "That's surprising and impressive."

"You should see her fight if you want to be impressed. She could literally walk into that living room right now and put any one of those men on his arse," Westlyn says.

Lorna laughs. "True story. She put Leith on his arse in the ring one time. To this day, he still won't talk about it."

Wow. Leith is not a small guy.

"Did your job as an agent bring you to Scotland?"

Bleu smiles. "In a roundabout way, it did."

"And you met Sin while you were on a job assignment here in Edinburgh?"

"Yes."

"That sounds like something out of a movie rather than real life."

"Our story would make a great novel."

"Maybe I should write it."

"You're an author?" Bleu asks.

I shrug. "Aspiring author."

"Writing and publishing a book must be exciting."

"I wouldn't know. I haven't completed one yet, but I can tell you that the writing process definitely isn't what everyone believes it to be." It's so damn hard.

"Are you working on anything now?"

"My most recent work in progress was a modern-day fairy tale. But I abandoned it."

The truth is that I haven't felt motivated to write

anything since my miscarriage. I open up my laptop and stare at the screen, but no words come into my mind.

"I've not been able to find time to write because our lives have been a whirlwind for the last several weeks. I'm still a student at uni, and I had to study for finals. And then we got married the Saturday before Christmas. It's been crazy busy for us."

"I've never seen him look so happy. We're absolutely thrilled for the two of you."

"That's sweet of you to say. Thank you."

"I'm sorry you're having these problems with Mina's family. No new bride should have to deal with that kind of problem in her marriage," Bleu says.

"I knew what kind of bullshit I was getting into when I married Hutch. None of this is unexpected."

"Which proves how strong you are," Bleu says.

"I think she's going to fit in perfectly with us," Ellison says.

I think so too. I feel comfortable with these women. Like they are my tribe.

23

MAXWELL HUTCHESON

Ava Rose's entrance into the world was nothing like this one. Mina's pregnancy reached the thirty-eight-week milestone and a cesarean section was done. My daughter was plucked from her mother's body and handed over to me. And I instantly became a father. It was exactly that cut and dried.

Ian's experience of becoming a father is much different from mine.

He and Shannon were asleep when her water broke. They rushed to the hospital believing that the baby could fall out at any minute. Needless to say, they were let down to learn she was dilated only two centimeters. That was hours ago. Per Ian's reports, the poor lass is in agony and exhausted. Still at two centimeters, they have little hope that the bairn will be born anytime soon.

All of us sit taller when Ian comes into the waiting room.

"Please tell us that poor lass has made some kind of progress," my mum says.

Ian shakes his head. "Still no change."

My mum sighs. "Have they given her anything for the pain?"

"She finally gave in and took something about ten minutes ago. She's resting, so I thought it would be a good time to step out and update you."

"Her mum is sitting with her?" my dad asks.

"Her mum and sister."

"You shouldn't worry, Ian. The same thing happened to me when I was in labor with Max. My water broke and I made no progress for hours and hours, and then all of a sudden the wee jobby decided to come. The doctor barely made it into the room in time for his delivery."

"She's becoming discouraged. She thought she'd be like the other women in her family and deliver the baby quickly."

"She shouldn't compare herself to other women. We're all different. Just keep encouraging her. Tell her to not give up. Tell her she can do it."

"I will, Mum." Ian sighs. "I should get back to her."

"We'll be right here, son. We aren't going anywhere."

Lou leans against me, resting her head against my upper arm. "Tired, mo maise?"

"I am."

I lift my arm and wrap it around her. "I've got you. Close your eyes and take a nap if you want. Sounds like we're going to be here a while."

"I don't think I can." She lowers her voice. "Every time I close my eyes, I remember being here."

I know it must be painful for her. "Do you want to leave?"

"No. I'll soon have new memories connected to this place. Happy memories to replace the sad ones."

"My brother is about to become a father to a wee one. I'm not sure if I should be proud or frightened."

"Ian will make a fine father."

Ian has matured a lot. "He'll be a better father than I was in the beginning. But then again, I'm not sure that's saying much. He wouldn't have to be very good to be a better father than I was."

"Don't say things like that."

"You have to admit that I was awful in the beginning."

"You were dreadful when we met, but that's not who you are today. You are a wonderful father to Ava Rose and she adores you."

"She adores you too, muh muh."

"I love that little girl so much."

"I know you do. She couldn't be blessed with a more loving mum."

I don't know if Mina would have been capable of loving Ava Rose the way Lou unconditionally loves her. Mina was a selfish woman. I believe she would have grown bored with a bairn after the new wore off. Spit-up and dirty nappies wouldn't have suited Mina's style.

Lou doesn't know yet, but I have plans for our family other than adding new members. I want her to be Ava Rose's mum. Her legal mother. And when our problems with the Lochridges are over, we're going to explore that possibility.

Darkness turns to light, and the sun turns into a moon again. I'm not sure how many hours it took, but baby Pearl has finally arrived.

The wee lassie is lying on Shannon's chest when

we enter the room, her head covered by a beanie. But Shannon and the baby aren't the ones who catch my attention. It's my brother. I can't remember ever seeing him look so happy.

"Isn't she grand?" Ian asks.

"Oh, she's a bonnie one," my dad says.

"The doctor and nurses told us that she looks healthy. And even if they hadn't, I'd know by looking at those cheeks."

"That's such a relief to hear. How do you feel, Shannon?" my mum asks.

"I'm exhausted. And sore. Very sore."

"As to be expected, but you'll feel better in no time at all." My mum leans closer for a better look at her new granddaughter and lifts the beanie. "Lots of dark hair, just like Ian when he was born."

"I'm glad she took after him. I was bald."

"I think she looks like me," Ian says and his voice reflects the pride and happiness he feels about his new daughter. And while I'm happy for him, I'm also envious.

Shannon insisted that Ian take a prenatal paternity test so he'd know without question that Pearl is his daughter. She didn't want him to ever have doubts about it. And he won't because the test proved he is the bairn's father.

Unlike me, Ian will see himself within his daughter. That's a precious gift that I'll never have in Ava Rose. But I won't love her less because of it.

When it's Lou's turn to hold Pearl, she takes her into her arms and holds her closely, pressing a kiss against the top of her beanie-covered head. She instantly shifts her weight back and forth between her feet, humming a soft melody, just as she does when she's trying to get Ava Rose to go to sleep.

Lou was born to be a mother.

She was born to be the mother of my children.

And I can't wait to give her what her heart longs for.

24

CAITRIONA HUTCHESON

Powerful people always have weaknesses and secrets. Usually big ones. You just have to find them. I haven't been able to get Bleu Breckenridge's words out of my head.

She said that I should make a list of facts and suspicions, and the two have a tendency to coincide, bringing the pieces of the puzzles together. That each piece will build upon the next.

The problem with that? I don't know the Lochridges. And I'm not sure Hutch truly does either. Not really. I believe those people have many secrets and they are buried deeply.

"What are you thinking so hard about, mo maise?"

I look up from my partially eaten breakfast. "I'm not sure you want to know the answer to that question."

"That answer makes me want to know even more."

"Did you know that Bleu Breckenridge was an FBI agent before she married Sin?"

"I did."

"The wives and I were discussing our problems with the Lochridges the other night, and they believe we need to put a stop to it before it has a chance to go to court."

"I would love nothing better. Believe me, I would if I knew how."

I'm going to toss this out there and see what Hutch says. "I think they were suggesting that we blackmail them so they won't seek custody of Ava Rose."

"Blackmailing a Lochridge?" Hutch shakes his head. "That's a terrible plan."

"Is it really?" I can't imagine anything being a terrible plan if it means we don't have to fight to keep Ava Rose.

"Aye, a very bad idea."

"You're banking everything on a judge giving Ava Rose to us because I've proven my character. And the truth is that simply may not happen."

"I know very well, Lou. It's on my mind night and day."

"There is no danger of losing Ava Rose if they don't sue for custody. We can assure that they don't if we gain the right kind of knowledge about them."

"I have knowledge about them. I know things about Thomas Lochridge that would send him to jail for a very long time, but we can never use any of it against him."

What is Hutch thinking? "We'd be crazy not to."

"What happens to my daughter when Thomas takes me down with him?"

"What does that mean?"

"If I rat him out, he'll never let me go free while he sits in jail. His life ends and so will mine."

Oh, I see. "Because you did illegal things for him?"

"That's another one of those questions that you shouldn't ask because I'm not going to give you the answer."

"I'm your wife."

"Aye, you are. And it's my job to protect you."

"I don't care what Thomas made you do. I'll always stand by you."

"I know you will, but knowing that kind of information is a burden I'll never place on you. I love you too much to do that to you."

I understand. I do. And that's why I too will not burden Hutch by telling him what I plan on doing to get us out of this colossal mess.

Hutch gets up from the table and comes to kiss me goodbye. "It's Monday. Are you cooking tonight?"

"I can if you want me to."

"I do."

"What would you like?"

"Mmm… surprise me."

I've had an idea simmering in the back of my mind for a while. "What time should I have dinner ready?"

He kisses my forehead and I melt. I do every time he does that. "I'll be home by six."

I go to the window and pull back the drape, watching the black luxury sedan disappear over the hill. For good measure, I wait a few more minutes to be sure that Hutch doesn't come back to the house before I make the call that will hopefully change this course we're currently on.

"Hi, Bleu. It's Cait Hutcheson. I know it's a bit early. I hope I haven't caught you at a bad time."

"No, it's fine. The kids just finished breakfast and they're watching their favorite show. How are you?"

"Not great."

"I'm sorry to hear that, but I'm not surprised."

"I'd really like to meet with you and talk more about what you said the other night. Are you free today or tomorrow?"

"I'm free today. Can you meet for lunch?"

"Absolutely."

"I have a good idea about what you'd like to discuss. I think you could benefit from having Shaw join us today. She has connections you would find helpful."

Bleu knows that I want to talk about the Lochridges? I suppose I shouldn't be surprised by that considering that she was once an FBI agent. She can probably smell motive from a mile away.

"And the other wives?" I'm willing to take help anywhere I can get it.

"Moral support. That's all you'll get from Elli, Westlyn, and Lorna."

"I could use a bit of that, actually."

"I have a feeling we're going to need to discuss this without the wrong ears being within earshot. Can you meet us at Duncan's Whisky Bar at noon?"

Duncan's Whisky Bar. I'm guessing that's Leith and Lorna's establishment.

"Noon would be perfect."

∼

I ENTER THE FRONT DOOR OF DUNCAN'S WHISKY BAR, and it looks like every other pub in Edinburgh but something—I'm not sure what—tells me that it is anything but ordinary.

Every man within the establishment turns and looks at me. At the same time, Bleu is out of her seat coming toward me. "I'm sorry they're acting as though they've never seen a woman before. You're a new face, and they're wondering why you're here."

I'm not sure what that means, and I'm afraid to ask after Hutch's statement regarding the Breckenridges.

"Come with me. We're sitting at the special table today."

I sit down and look at the table. Looks like a normal table to me. "What makes it special?"

The women look at each other and laugh. And I realize that I may have made a mistake by asking. "I'm sorry. I shouldn't have asked that."

"It's okay. Don't worry about it."

Whatever makes the table special remains a mystery because she doesn't offer a reason. But I know who I'm sharing a table with right now.

The Bella Mafia.

"It's barely noon and I'm having a whisky. I don't give a damn. I deserve one after the weekend I had with Sinclair Breckenridge's sons."

"Ooh, my nephews must have been very bad if you're calling them Sin's sons."

"They're mine when they behave. They're his when they show their little asses."

Bleu lifts her hand and a waitress comes over immediately. "What can I get for you?"

"Johnny Walker Black Label. Make it a double."

"Rusty Nail for me," Ellison says. "Westlyn?"

"Sauvignon blanc."

Shaw nods. "That sounds good. I'll have a sauvignon blanc too."

"Scotch fizz," Lorna says. "And tell Kenrick to make it my way. He'll know what you mean."

"Tomatin. And you can make mine a double as well," I tell the waitress. I'm going to need more than a single for what I'm here to talk about.

"A woman after my own heart," Bleu says.

"Well, I am half-Scottish so a part of me should be able to drink whisky."

"I'm half-Scottish too. My mother was American but my father was a Scotsman."

"Same with me."

"Something else we have in common."

I toss back the last of my whisky, and I'm feeling a little braver about bringing up my reason for asking the wives to meet me. So I go for it. "I'm strong enough to stand alone. But I'm also smart enough to know when I need help, and I'm brave enough to ask for it. And I need your help."

"What kind of help?" Bleu asks.

"I'm actually not sure." I toy with the wet napkin beneath my whisky glass, tearing it into small pieces.

"We can't help you if you don't know what kind of help you need."

"Hutch has told me I can never ask him about the Breckenridges. He's only told me that you're loyal and trustworthy. And that's what I need—people I can trust. People who know how to keep secrets."

Bleu's brow lifts. "Secrets where the Lochridges are concerned?"

"Yes. And if you are who I think you are, you're

the only people I know who have the power to help me."

"I'm not going to ask who you believe we are, and you're not going to tell us. Once those words are spoken, they can never be unspoken. Do you understand?"

"I do."

"Who we are is something we'll never speak of again."

"Understood."

I may not know exactly who these women are, but I do know one thing: Bleu is the leader.

"Is there more to your troubles with the Lochridges than we've discussed?"

This is it. I have to confide in these women if I hope to gain their help. "There's more. Much more."

"We need to know all of the facts if we're to help you."

Mina's betrayal. Ava Rose's paternity. Blair's threat. Hutch's job. I tell the wives—the Bella Mafia as I call them in my mind—everything I know from beginning to end.

Bleu shakes her head. "Mina left Max in one hell of a mess, which is also your mess now."

"Tell me about it."

"I'm sorry to hear that you and Max have been going through this. It must be awful living with the fear that they will try to take the baby from you."

"We love her so much and we're terrified we'll lose her to those horrible people because they're blood relation."

"I didn't give birth to my daughter, but she is mine. I'm a mama bear who would rip apart anyone who tried to take Lourdes away from me."

"Then you understand how we feel about Ava Rose and where we're coming from."

"One hundred percent. And that's why I'm going to help you find a way to keep that little girl."

"*We're* going to help you," Shaw says.

"Hutch has seen a family law solicitor and has been advised about the legal way to handle this situation. But I don't think it's going to work with these people. They don't fight fairly."

"I know you both must hate it, but it's wise for Max to keep Blair appeased for the time being. It buys the time you'll need for what we have to do. And speaking of what we have to do... how far are you willing to go to end this with the Lochridges?"

Blair made the decision to fuck with me. She went for my throat because she believes she is the stronger one.

She is wrong.

Hutch and Ava Rose are my world. My happiness. My joy.

My beautiful ever after.

I won't allow her to rob me of that.

"I will cut that bitch off at the knees and smile while I do it."

Ellison bursts into laughter. "A Southern girl ready to cut a bitch. That's what I'm talking about. She's definitely one of us now."

Unlike Ellison, there's no amusement on Bleu's face. She's dead serious. "You'd go that far? No hesitation at all?"

"I've never had anything in my life worth fighting for until Hutch and Ava Rose. So yes, I would go to hell and back for them. No question. No hesitation."

"I believe you. And Max and Ava Rose are very lucky to have you in their life."

"Can you help me?" Even I hear the desperation in my voice.

"I believe we can work together and solve this problem. But you can never ask the ins and outs of what we do or how we do it."

"I understand one hundred percent."

Bleu looks at Shaw. "We'll need your connection."

"That won't be a problem, but I'll need to know who we're targeting? Blair? Thomas? Both?"

"What are your thoughts, Cait?" Bleu asks.

"Blair for now. If we don't get what we need through her, we'll move on to Thomas."

Shaw nods. "I think that's a good plan. Ending your problem with Blair could prevent later complications with Thomas. She should be dealt with first and we possibly eliminate our problem with half the work."

"Valid point. And a satisfying way to end this, I'm sure."

They don't know the half of it. "I can't lie. Taking her down is going to feel great."

"My connection will begin by hacking into Blair's emails, her social media, her bank accounts. Everything will be scoured for information we can use against her."

The woman I was a year ago would never have contemplated invading someone's privacy. She wouldn't have considered blackmailing anyone to get what she wants. But I'm a different woman today than even yesterday. I'm the kind of woman that you want to go to war beside. Not against. And Blair will not question that when I'm finished with her.

Make no mistake about it. She's going to regret fucking with me and mine.

"How long does something like that take?"

"My connection is thorough. He pores over the information with a fine toothcomb, so it could be a few days."

"That's much faster than I expected."

"This nightmare will be over for you and Max very soon. I promise."

I believe Bleu.

"I want you all to know how grateful I am. I don't know how I could possibly ever repay you, but if there's anything I can do for you, all you have to do is ask."

"Max has been good to us over the years. We're happy to help any way we can. There is no debt with us."

Shit. I left out an important detail. "That's great to hear... except Max can't know about this."

"Are you sure that's best? Keeping something so important from your husband?"

"Hutch wants to be a good example for Ava Rose by doing what is right. I respect my husband for wanting to do the honorable thing, but it isn't going to win this battle with the Lochridges. I firmly believe that we must do what is necessary in this instance, right or wrong, if we're to be good examples for her later."

The wives voice their agreement at the same time.

"You're a strong woman who is choosing to take control of this situation and do what needs to be done for your family. Ava Rose couldn't be in better hands."

Bleu respects what I'm doing. I see it in her eyes.

Hutch may be angry with me for doing this behind his back, but I truly believe in my heart that it's the only way to end this. I hope he's able to see that I'm doing this out of my love for him and Ava Rose.

Everything I do is for them.

25

MAXWELL HUTCHESON

Damn, something smells good.

I love Monday nights. Very little compares to coming home from a long day at the office to a delicious Cajun meal cooked by my wife. She is an excellent chef.

"Hutch?" she calls out.

I place my briefcase on the table beside the door leading out to the garage. "Aye, it's me."

"Don't come into the kitchen. Go around the other way."

That's odd. She's never asked me to do that before. "Any special reason I must go that way?"

"I have a surprise and I'm not ready for you to see it."

Hmm… a surprise? "Where should I go?"

"Wait for me in the dining room. I'll be there in a minute to serve you."

To serve me? Fuck, I don't hate the way that sounds. "I'm hungry. Don't keep me waiting for long or I'll come for you."

"Oh, I know you will."

I take my seat at the head of the table and contemplate what in the world my wife is up to. She's never made me bypass the kitchen and go into the dining room without seeing her.

What is that wee vixen up to?

Lou comes into the dining room, and I inspect her from head to toe as she walks toward me.

White lace see-through apron trimmed with black satin ribbon. Black sash tied around her waist. Black garters and hose. No bra. No knickers. I can easily see her rosy pink nipples and that wee strip of hair between her legs that I love so much.

"Fuck, Lou."

"A whisky before dinner?"

"Aye."

She places a glass on the table in front of me. "Three fingers?"

I may ask her that same question later.

"Aye. Please."

She pours my whisky and places the bottle on the table.

"I hope you're hungry."

"I am indeed. Where is everyone?"

"I sent everyone home except for Mrs. McVey. She's with Ava Rose in the nursery. I asked her to stay over and take care of her tonight."

"They're in the nursery now?"

"Yes."

"Then come here."

I reach out, grabbing her around the waist, and pull her onto my lap.

"What do you think you're doing?"

My chest vibrates when I chuckle. "Well, if you don't know then I'm not doing it right."

Grasping the back of her neck, I pull her closer and our mouths open simultaneously. Her tongue meets mine and I taste a hint of whisky. "Mmm… someone has already had some water of life?"

"Maybe."

"It's not like you to drink whisky without me."

"I was with friends."

"Rachel?"

"No. Bleu and the other wives."

"How many drinks did you have?"

"One whisky turned into two. And two turned into three."

"Are you smashed?"

"No, but I feel pretty good."

"You feel pretty good, aye?"

"Mmm-hmm."

She parts her legs when my hand moves up her inner thigh. "Do you know what I want to do to you right now?"

"I'm not sure but I know it involves allowing dinner to get cold."

"Aye, mo maise. Dinner is going to be cold when I'm finished with you."

Standing, I lift Lou's body with mine and lower her bum to the table. "You'll never look at this table again without remembering what I'm about to do to you on top of it."

I'm impatient to fuck my wife on top of this table, but my body must be content with delayed gratification. My wife comes before me.

She trembles and her breath increases when I trail my fingers down her stomach, dipping them into her navel, and stroking that thin strip of hair over her groin. Petting her. "Such an appetizing pussy you have, Mrs. Hutcheson."

Lou squirms beneath me, her bottom lip held prisoner by her upper teeth. "Taste me."

"Patience, mo maise."

There'll be no instant gratification for either of us. I'm going to make this last.

She moans as my mouth follows the same path my fingers just took, my wet tongue—in place of my finger—dipping into her navel this time.

"You take great joy in teasing me," she whispers.

"Patience, my love. I'm going to give you what you want."

"I know you will. You always do."

I drop to my knees and push her thighs apart, taking a brief moment to appreciate the shiny, swollen pink beauty between my wife's legs. I love that it's mine. Only mine. No other man gets to see it, smell it, touch it, or taste it.

I inhale deeply, taking in her intoxicating scent. I swear that there's nothing in the world like it. It's unique only to her, and my cock instantly reacts to the fragrance because he also knows it well.

"Are you trying to kill me or what, Hutch?"

"I told you, love. Patience."

Her body jolts when I barely touch her clit with the tip of my finger. "Someone is extra sensitive this evening."

"Yes."

Applying a little more pressure, I rotate my finger in a circle at the top of her slit, massaging that tiny little erect protrusion of skin and nerves. "Is that what you want, Lou?"

The bottom of her feet land on top of my shoulders and her toes dig into the flesh. "Oh God. You are so good at that."

"My mouth is jealous. He wants his turn."

"By all means, give it to him."

I lower my head between her legs and drag my tongue upward, taking special care of her clit with the stiffened tip. Her body vibrates like a leaf trembling in a soft wind.

"Mmm... mmm... mmm."

I don't need to hear validation through words from Lou. Her sexy sounds tell me everything I need to hear: when to give it to her harder, when to move faster. And right now, her sounds are telling me that she is close to the edge. But I'm not going to let it happen just yet. Because I want to hear her beg for it.

I stop and look up at her writhing on the table, deliberately leaving my mouth close enough for her to feel my warm breath.

"Hutch! What are you doing?"

"Just slowing things down a bit."

"I don't want you to slow things down. Keep going. I'm so close to coming." I hear the desperation in her voice. And I love it.

"Beg me."

"What?"

"You heard me. Beg for your orgasm."

Lou pushes her fingers into the top of my hair. "Please, Hutch. I'm going to lose it if you don't start back."

I lick her a few more times, enough to reinitiate what was already there. "Go ahead. Keep begging me for it."

Lou's upper body props against the table and

she looks down, watching me. And that mouth of hers. It's a perfect O while she watches me eat her out.

"Make me come. Please, Hutch. I want it so badly. I need it. I'll die if you don't give it to me."

I take her to the peak of her orgasm and her entire body spasms, shuddering and twisting from her intense release. And then I'm rewarded with a flood of sweet nectar on my tongue.

I get up from my knees and stand, looking down at the shattered mess I've made of my wife.

Her eyes on mine. Her mouth smiling. Her every muscle relaxed.

Absolute contentment. That's what I see laid before me on the table.

I open my hand and place it against the space between her breasts. It isn't quite over her heart, but I can still feel the pounding just to the right.

I drag my hand down until it's splayed over her flat stomach. My palm and outstretched fingers look so big against the backdrop of her small frame. And I find myself wondering what she'll look like as her belly grows with our child.

"Tell me what you're thinking," she says, her voice soft and low.

Now isn't the time for that conversation. "Ask me later. Right now, I want you to wrap your legs around me so I can fuck you."

She smiles and lifts her legs, locking them behind my arse. "Anything you want."

I bring my palms down against the sides of her hips, making a smacking sound. "That's what I like to hear out of my obedient wife."

I position my cock at her entrance and lower my

upper body to hers because I want to hear her gasp against my ear when I shove my cock inside of her.

That sexy, breathy sound on the first thrust. There's nothing like it.

"Ahh."

Hell yeah. There it is. I love hearing that sharp intake of air so fucking much.

I rise and watch Lou's face while I move inside of her. Her green-brown eyes are locked on mine, and I know in my heart that no woman has or ever will consume me the way she does. "You have my heart, my soul, everything that makes me who I am. It's all yours."

"As I am yours."

I feel something with Lou that I never felt without her.

Complete.

26

CAITRIONA HUTCHESON

YOU KNOW HOW IT FEELS WHEN YOU WALK INTO A spider web and the more you try to pick the web off, the stickier it becomes? I'm going to be the spider who spins the web that is going to stick to Blair. Only she isn't going to be able to free herself. The harder she fights to be rid of me, the more my web and I are going to cling to her.

And what I find most satisfying? I'm an underestimated predator she won't see coming.

Bleu, Shaw, and I enter Bleu's—I'm not sure what to call it. Office? That doesn't feel like the right word. Evidence room? Maybe. That feels like a better fit.

Photos attached to a wall. Colored strings tied from one pin to another forming a rainbow web. Stacks of papers on the table in the middle of the room.

"Wow. I've never seen anything like this."

"You can never tell anyone about this room or the things you see while you're in it. We're allowing you to be here because you're Max's wife and we have business. We're placing our trust in you as an extension of the trust we have in him. It would be the worst decision of your life to betray us."

Fuck. I think my safety—maybe my life—was just threatened. "I understand and I will never tell anyone."

"Good. Now that we have that out of the way, let's get down to it."

Shaw pushes a stack of papers in front of me at least eight inches high. "My connection hit the golden jackpot of filth on that bitch. You can have your pick of how you want to blackmail her."

"What is all of this?"

"Copies of her texts, emails, private messages on social media platforms… and on dating websites."

"She's posing as a single woman?"

Shaw laughs. "She's posing as something, but it's not a single white female."

"Then what?"

Bleu places a photo of a man on the table and pushes it toward me. "Do you know this man?"

Dark hair, a little thin on top. Brown eyes. The man is handsome—very handsome in fact—but I can't recall ever seeing him. "He doesn't look familiar to me."

"His name is Roman Kirk. He and Mina connected a few months before she was in the car accident."

Could he be Ava Rose's father?

I look at the photo again, searching for any similarities between the two. It's impossible to see anything when Ava Rose looks so much like Mina.

"Wait, I'm confused. You found these messages between Mina and this man on Blair's computer?"

"Yes. There are thousands of them," Shaw says.

Wow. Blair was helping Mina cheat on Hutch?

"Everything that you're thinking right now is wrong. The messages on Blair's computer weren't Mina's to him. They were Roman Kirk's to her."

I'm not following. "I'm sorry. I need you to explain what this means."

"It's confusing, we know," Bleu says and gestures to Shaw. "She's about to explain everything."

"There can only be two possible explanations. One would be that Blair knows the man and she was allowing him to use her computer. It's completely possible but very unlikely. The second option, which is the one that I'm leaning toward, would be that Blair was online impersonating this man."

Like catphishing? "You think Blair was messaging with Mina and pretending to be this man?"

"There are thousands of messages between Mina and this man at all times of the day and night using her IP address. I absolutely believe that she was pretending to be this man."

"Why would Blair do that to Mina?"

"If we knew the answer to that question then we'd probably know why Blair transferred ten thousand pounds into the man's account."

I can't believe I'm about to say this. "Blair is filthier than I expected."

"Blair left us a great online trail, and it proves many things, but it's just an outline. You'll have to go see Roman Kirk if you want to hear the full story."

Bleu rejoins the conversation. "And I suspect you'll need to take plenty of cash when you do. I have a feeling this man isn't going to spill the beans free of charge. Do you have readily available cash without asking Max for it?"

"I have my own money." Thank God.

"Enough to pay this man off?"

"I have more than enough to buy his version of the story."

"That's good."

"I don't want to do this alone." I'm scared. And I'm scared to admit that I'm scared.

"There's no way in hell that we'd let you do this alone," Bleu says.

Shaw nods. "For sure. Not even a chance."

"You have no idea how much I appreciate your support. I don't have a lot of friends. Only one really."

"I'm speaking on behalf of everyone, and I hope they don't mind my saying so, but you have five new friends in Shaw, Ellison, Lorna, Westlyn, and myself."

"That makes me really happy to hear. Thank you."

I've never really been one for making friends. As a child and adolescent, I was too embarrassed to bring friends home. I didn't want them to see my mom drunk or strung out. And after I came to live with Heidi and my dad, I was still ashamed. I didn't want anyone to see how unloved and unwanted I was by my own dad and stepmother.

I had one friend when I was a child in New Orleans, and then I was friendless until I met Rachel at The Last Drop. We've been peas and carrots ever since.

"Can you get the money today?" Bleu asks.

"I can get it within the hour."

"Then I say that we do this today."

Man, it would be wonderful to not worry about Blair anymore. Hutch and I could finally announce our marriage. No more hiding as though we're the ones doing wrong.

"I'm ready to put this to bed for good. Let's do this."

Bleu bites her bottom lip and fist pumps the air. "Hell yes. This is going to be fun."

She goes to the desk, opens the drawer—and holy shit—takes out a handgun. "Don't be afraid, Cait. I'm only taking my baby as a precaution."

Her baby?

They're Bella Mafia, Cait. And Bleu is a former FBI agent. Of course, she carries a gun. What did you expect?

Bleu cocks the gun and looks down the chamber. At least that's what I think she's doing. I really have no idea. "Do you shoot?"

"No."

"You should let me teach you sometime. And I can also teach you how to defend yourself."

"I know basic self-defense."

"I can teach you so much more than the basics."

"I would love that. Thank you."

~

ROMAN KIRK WORKS IN A KILTMAKER SHOP?

A. Kiltmaker. Shop. Yes, it's one of the fancier shops where they tailor fit the customer and charge an outrageous price. But still, he spends his days catering to Scotsmen who see themselves as better than him.

The whole thing is so damn puzzling. From what I know about Mina, I can't see her being with a man like him no matter how good-looking he is.

"Good afternoon. How may I help you?"

"Are you Roman Kirk?"

"I am."

"My name is Cait and I'm hoping you can help me. I have some questions about Mina. But more specifically about her sister Blair."

His pleasant expression fades. "I have nothing to say about either of them."

I remove an envelope from my jacket pocket. "Would the stack of money in this envelope motivate you to have something to say about them?"

"It would help. But I'm working right now." He looks at the front of the store and then plucks a kilt from a rack, pretending to show it to us. "That isn't a conversation I can have here and now. I'm engaged to be married to the owner's daughter, so you can see how that might be a sensitive topic."

"Can you meet us after work?"

He returns the kilt to the rack. "My shift ends at five. Name a place and I'll be there."

I look at Bleu for a suggestion since I have no idea what makes a good location for a meeting like this.

"We'll wait for you at The Landing Strip on High Riggs. We'll be there at 5:30. The three of us and that envelope of money will be gone by 5:35 if you don't show."

Command, strength, power. The three ooze from Bleu's voice.

One shouldn't toy with Bleu. That's very evident. And I'm relieved to have her on my side. Hell, I'm relieved to have all of the Bella Mafia on my side. Those five women are to be feared.

"You don't have to worry. I'll be there."

We leave the shop and it's only a minute until Bleu's driver arrives to get us.

"I want to go to The Landing Strip about as much as I want to eat glass," Shaw says.

"I know it's sleazy, but it's safe because it'll be occupied by friends of our husbands."

"Someone tell me what The Landing Strip is."

"They call it a gentlemen's club, but it's actually a place where men, who are not actually gentlemen, go to watch topless dancing." Bleu frowns and point to her stomach and crotch. "You know. That kind of landing strip."

"Ohhh, I see now." Gross.

"It's a very seedy place that exploits women. There's no doubt about that, but there is zero risk associated with meeting him there. I can call ahead, reserve the VIP room and leave instructions for him to be searched at the door."

Bleu is completely confident in her ability to call this club, book a room, and give orders to the men working there.

Damn. That's badass.

"You think Roman Kirk could be dangerous?" Shaw asks.

"I don't think he's dangerous in a physical aspect, but we certainly have reason to not trust him. If my suspicions are right, he could be capable of doing something worse than physical harm if given the opportunity. We can't be too careful with this man."

I'm trying to gather enough courage to ask Bleu about her suspicions when Shaw closes the door of opportunity. "I say we go over to Duncan's and have a drink while we wait for the kiltmaker to finish his shift."

"I could go for a whisky." Or three. Hutch wouldn't complain. He loved what followed my drinking excursion with the Bella Mafia a few nights ago.

"I should probably text my husband."

"You haven't changed your mind about telling him what you're doing?"

"No way. I may be a new wife, but this is a clear case of forgiveness being easier to obtain than permission."

> **LOU:** I'll be late tonight. I'm out with Bleu and Shaw.
> **HUTCH:** Having drinks?
> **LOU:** Maybe.
> **HUTCH:** Can I fuck you on top of the table when you get home?
> **LOU:** I was thinking we'd do something else. Maybe make out in the backseat of the Benz.
> **HUTCH:** By "make out" you mean fuck, right?
> **LOU:** We'll see.
> **HUTCH:** Yeah, trust me. You mean fuck.
> **LOU:** OK.
> **HUTCH:** Have a good time. Love you.
> **LOU:** Love you too.

I feel a little bit bad about doing this behind Hutch's back but not bad enough to change my mind about going through with it. In the end, we're going to win against the Lochridges, and he's not going to remember how we got there. I hope.

Three whiskies later, I'm feeling looser. Braver. "I don't know about you, ladies, but I'm full-on ready to interrogate the kiltmaker."

"That's my girl."

"It's almost time. We should probably be making our way over to the not-so-gentlemanly club."

We enter the club and the first thing I see is a young woman on stage dancing around a pole. She's topless and wearing only a tiny G-string. I'm not sure why she bothered with the scrap of fabric. It leaves nothing to the imagination when she parts her legs. And these men are loving it.

Making the decision to become an escort was painful for me, but the choice to do this must have been a gut-wrenching decision for this woman. Surely, she didn't choose this profession because she had other options.

Poor thing.

I'm puzzled by the way the men react when they see us walking through the club. Catcalls. Whistles. Pinches or pats on the ass. I expected any of those things, or all of them, but these men are lowering their heads.

Bowing.

Bowing to show respect to these members of the Bella Mafia.

Bowing to their queen.

Nothing has ever been clearer.

"Good evening, Randall."

The man lowers his head. "Good evening, missus. The VIP room has been prepared for you."

Prepared for you. I wonder what that consists of. A

good cleaning with bleach, I hope. Twice for good measure.

The man leads us to the room and wow. Just wow. Elegant red damask wallpaper. Luxurious red leather tufted sofas. Rich red and gold carpet. Warm, glowing light dancing around the room from the flame inside of the fireplace. It's gorgeous. And I'd want to bring Hutch to this room if it weren't inside of this vile-ass club.

Damn. I wonder if my husband has ever been in this room.

I probably shouldn't wonder about that. Or ever ask.

"Shall I bring your guest back when he arrives?"

"That would be perfect. And do ensure that he is thoroughly searched at the door."

I walk the room inspecting the décor, touching nothing. "This room is quite lovely. It's unexpected compared to what it looks like out there."

"It is lovely, but its beauty will never mask all of the ugly that happens inside of these four walls."

I wholeheartedly agree with that.

The door opens and Roman Kirk is led into the room by a man who is every bit as large as Raith who guards the entrance into Inamorata. "Will you be requiring my presence?"

Bleu pats her hip. Her gun. "No, Seamus. We'll be fine."

"I'll be readily available if I'm needed."

"Thank you."

Roman Kirk looks at Bleu, and then Shaw, and then me. "Who are you people?"

"Who we are is not important. And it's definitely

not the reason you're here." Bleu gestures to the sofa. "Take a seat. We have lots to discuss."

He moves to the sofa across from us and sits, his legs spreading wide, and his kilt falls between them. "You said there was money?"

I remove the envelope from my jacket and toss it at him. "Twenty thousand pounds. It's yours if you give me the answers I want. If you don't, you're not walking out of here with a single pound of that money."

"What do you want to know?"

"How do you know Blair?"

"I met her at the shop when she came in with her husband for a custom kilt. She returned to the shop later without him and told me that she'd give me two hundred pounds if I'd let her take my picture. I thought it was odd but I needed the money, so I allowed her to photograph me with her mobile."

"When did you see her again?"

"She came back about a month later."

"What did she want the next time you saw her?"

"She had created a profile on a dating website using my name and picture. I was pissed off about it and demanded that she take it down. She told me that she couldn't and wouldn't. And that's when she offered me a thousand pounds to let her continue using my name and profile on the site. I didn't want to do it, but I work at a kiltmaker shop. I don't earn that much."

"Are you aware that she was pretending to be you while she was messaging back and forth with a woman from the dating site?"

"Aye."

"What happened next?"

"She asked me to meet the woman. Mina. And I got more money for taking her out on a date."

"How many times did Blair pay you to see Mina?"

"I couldn't put a number on it. It was many times."

"Did you have a sexual relationship with Mina?"

"It became sexual."

"Because you wanted it to or because Blair paid you to?"

He hesitates a moment. "Mina wasn't my type. She was a rich bitch just like the customers I deal with every day. I didn't like her at all, but I couldn't turn down that kind of money."

"Did you make her believe you loved her?"

"Aye. That's what I was paid to do."

"Did Blair ever tell you why she orchestrated a fake relationship between you and her sister?"

"She never told me why and I didn't ask. Because I didn't care."

"What happened the last time you saw Mina?"

"She told me she was going to have my baby and I was aff my heid. I told her everything about how I'd been paid by Blair to be her pretend boyfriend. She ran out of my flat and I haven't seen her since. That was almost two years ago, and I've been biding my time, waiting for her to show up with a bairn on her hip."

"Mina isn't going to be showing up. She's dead."

His eyes widen. "What happened to her?"

"She got into a car accident after she left you."

"So there's no baby after all?" He reaches up and runs his hands through the top of his hair. "Thank fuck for that. I can't believe I've been so damn worried all this time."

This guy is thrilled because he believes his child died with Mina in that car accident. And I don't feel one bit of regret or remorse for what I'm about to do. "You're off the hook. There's no baby."

"I was scared when you showed up asking about Blair and Mina, but this is great news." He picks up the envelope. "Plus, I made another twenty thousand pounds. This is fucking grand."

What. A. Dick.

I want to yank that envelope out of his hand and beat the fuck out of him with it. And I may yet if he doesn't get out of my sight.

"I think we're done here."

"You're sure? No more questions?" Bleu asks.

I don't think I could bear to hear him say another word that dismisses Ava Rose as though she never mattered. "I'm satisfied with the information I've gotten."

He stands and shoves the envelope of money inside his jacket. "It's been a pleasure."

The three of us are quiet for a moment after he leaves. I think we're all a little sickened by what he had to say.

Bleu sighs. "I didn't like Mina, but I wouldn't have wished that on her."

Shaw places her hand over her heart. "Can you imagine how she must have been feeling after hearing that? It's no wonder that she got into an accident."

Her sister had betrayed her, and the man she loved turned out to be a phony who didn't want their child. Those were her final thoughts before she died. I almost wonder if she had the accident on purpose.

I feel sorry for Mina. And I feel numb on her behalf. "That was so much worse than I expected."

"Blair is an even more horrible person than we suspected," Shaw says.

"Blair is the one who planted the idea in Mina's head about the dating website. She suggests it in her texts over and over. And after hearing what Roman Kirk had to say, I think Blair talked Mina into doing the dating website so she would be lured away from Max instead of trying to reconcile with him. And that means Blair would have him all to herself."

Bleu's theory makes total sense.

"This wasn't a simple plan. It was intricate. She didn't come up with this overnight. The way you choose to handle this matter must be carefully planned. You can't give Blair any wiggle room."

Shaw's right. I must corner her without any chance of escape.

"I understand you have to hold on to this information in order to blackmail her, but it's a shame you don't get to expose what she's done," Bleu says.

"I know. It's a shame I can't do both."

"Hiding Ava Rose's existence from Roman Kirk is the right thing to do. Don't ever question that."

I'm glad Bleu agrees. Not everyone would be of the same opinion.

"I would ordinarily say that a father has the right to know about his child but not in this case. Not him." Not that dick.

"He could potentially use her as a way to extort money out of you and Max. It's better that he doesn't know about her existence."

If he doesn't know she exists, he can never sue for custody.

"You don't have to convince me to not feel guilty about lying to him. I don't, not even a little." I can live with that lie for the sake of my baby girl.

27

MAXWELL HUTCHESON

"Your one o'clock is already here," Mary says.

Ah, fuck. I forgot about that last-minute schedule adjustment. "Remind me again who my one o'clock is."

"Ina Morata."

"Inamorata?" I chuckle as I say the word. Not because I'm amused but because I'm astounded.

"No. She pronounced it as Ina… Morata." Mary looks up at me and scowls. "Is something wrong with that name? I think it's lovely."

No one is named Ina Morata. That's what's wrong with it.

"Nothing's wrong with it. Where is Miss Morata?"

"I sent her into your office. I didn't know you were going to be so late coming back from lunch."

"Are you scolding me, Mary?"

"If I am it's because you need it."

"I tell you what. I'll try to do better, just for you."

"Aye right. I've heard that before, you rascal."

Mary is a delightful woman. She reminds me of my mum in so many ways. Probably because she treats me very much like a son. I'm going to miss her when I'm gone from here. I hope she's treated well by these arrogant assholes.

She gestures to my office door. "Go on. The bonnie lass has already been waiting for you too long."

I'm eager to see what is going on with Miss Ina Morata. Nothing about that name is coincidental.

Could it be Cora? Another inamorata?

I open my office door and the woman is sitting in one of the chairs facing my desk. My eyes are drawn to the back of her long, straight blond hair and my first thought is that it's Cora. But then I remember that Cora's hair isn't that long. Or platinum blond.

"My apologies, Miss Morata. I'm sorry to keep you waiting."

"Being made to wait implies that your time is more important than mine. And I assure you that my time is very important. And expensive. Ask any of my clients and they'll tell you so."

Her accent is strange. Is she faking a Scottish burr?

"I assure you I'm not under the impression that your time is less important than mine or anyone else's." I come around the chair and offer my hand. "It's a pleasure to make your acquaint—"

Green-brown hazel eyes. Long lashes. Nose adorned with a few scattered freckles.

Perfect. Red. Lips.

My wife.

My wife wearing a platinum blond wig?

"What are you doing?" I whisper.

"Are you expecting anyone?"

"Not that I'm aware of. I'm scheduled with *Miss Morata* until two o'clock."

"Good. Go sit down behind your desk, Mr. Hutcheson."

Lou gets up, walks over to the door, and locks it before coming to stand in front of me. She lowers herself to the floor and kneels between my legs, reaching for the buckle of my belt. "I'm going to suck you so hard."

Oh fuuuck yes.

I reach out and grip the wig, pulling it off her head. "I want that, but I also want you to look like my wife while you do it."

She smiles up at me while she lowers my zipper. "You don't want to see the back of a blonde's head bobbing up and down your cock?"

"Definitely not."

Lou pushes her fingers into my waistband. I lift my hips and she pulls down my trousers and Y-fronts, leaving them around my ankles.

She places her palms on my thighs and glides them upward until her fingertips brush my bollocks. She teases them for a moment, lightly sweeping her fingers back and forth beneath the bottom of my sac. Blood rushes toward my cock—filling, lengthening, thickening it. The ropes of veins are stiff and standing out.

"Fuck, you're being a tease."

The tip of her pink tongue darts out between her ruby red lips, licking them. "Am I?"

"Aye. A big one."

She grasps the base and I watch as her tongues circles around the head. My erection jolts each time her tongue moves over that sensitive area just below the crown. And then she licks away the little pearl on the tip.

Fuck. Me.

She alternates licking my length and circling her tongue around the head's edge before taking it fully into her mouth. "That feels so fucking good."

I grip her hair, pulling all of it into a ponytail, and I watch as her head bobs up and down. "I love seeing those red lips wrapped around my cock."

Tilting her head, she wraps her mouth around the side and moves up and down the shaft, her eyes locked on mine. "Every man on this planet wishes he had a wife like you. I am so lucky to call you mine."

Opening her mouth wider, she takes one of my bollocks in. She lightly sucks and releases while massaging it with her tongue. And then she does something that no one has ever done to me before, even Lou.

Something new. Something unexpected. Something both breathtaking and erotic.

Applying pressure beneath my sac, she rotates her finger in a circular motion. Slow, and then fast. Soft, and then hard.

And. Holy. Fuck.

I've never felt any-fucking-thing in the world like it.

"You've got to stop, mo maise. You're going to make me come."

She stops sucking and looks up at me. "I was going to let you come in my mouth and watch me swallow it."

Such filthy words coming out of such a beautiful

mouth. So filthy that they almost send me over the edge.

"Another time, mo maise. Definitely. Right now, I want to be inside of you. I have something else in mind."

I help Lou stand and I kick out of my shoes and trousers. Taking her hand, I lead her to the sofa. Without being told what to do next, she climbs on top of me.

I cradle her face with my hands. "My beautiful inamorata."

"You want to fuck your inamorata right here on the couch like this?"

"Aye. And then every time I look over at this sofa, I'll smile and remember how hard you rode my cock today."

She touches her fingers to my bottom lip. "Do you want me to take off my dress?"

"Aye." I love seeing her tits bounce.

She leans back and crosses her arms, gripping the bottom of her dress, and pulls upward. Fuck, she's naked beneath it.

"Not a stitch of clothing under your dress. I like that, Miss Morata."

"I thought you might."

I push my fingers back and forth through her wet slit, spreading her slick juices. "Slide this sweet wet pussy down my cock and ride it. Ride it until we both come."

She rises on her knees and with my tip positioned at her entrance, she lowers herself. I'm sheathed to the hilt by her pussy, and she's filled to her womb with my cock.

She fists the top of my hair and pulls, forcing my

face up. We stare at each other for at least ten heart-beats before she releases her hold and presses her forehead against mine. I feel like she's going to say something—something important—but no words come out.

Instead, she rises and plunges down again, rolling her hips forward and taking me deep into her pussy. With my hips thrusting upward, we perfect our rhythm, and I use my grip on her hips to pull her down onto my cock.

With every thrust, the couch bumps the wall but I can't stop. And I can't bring myself to give a fuck who hears what we're doing. Being inside her feels so damn good.

Stretching upward, I kiss her mouth. "I love you."

"I love you too. And I'd do anything for you. For us. For our family."

Our family. Fuck, I love hearing her say that.

I wrap my arms around her waist and hold her tightly as I thrust into her one final time, emptying myself inside of her. And one of these days I'm going to do that with a beautiful purpose behind it.

We become motionless and I hold Lou tightly. I soon feel the ooze of warm cum dripping out of her but neither of us moves a muscle.

"Miss Morata, you are my new favorite client."

"I better be the only client who rides your cock."

"I have a few who ride my arse but none ride my cock. I leave that to you."

"That's good to know."

"I'm happy you're here but what made you decide to put on a disguise and come to the firm?"

"I'm your wife and I've never seen where you

work. Plus, I also thought it would be fun to fool around right under everyone's nose."

"I'm not sure how sneaky we were just now. I'm pretty sure the entire third floor just heard us shagging."

"Even better. Let 'em speculate about what you were doing with your new client."

My phone rings and I groan. "I have to answer that. And quickly." I don't need Mary wondering why it takes numerous rings for me to pick up. "Aye?"

"Your two o'clock has arrived early."

Fucking great.

"Miss Morata and I are finalizing some details."

"Also, Blair is here. She's asking if she can see you briefly before your next client."

Fuck. Fuck. Fuck.

"If my next client is already here then I won't be able to see her."

"She's—" Mary lowers her voice. "*Insisting*."

Of fucking course, she is. It's what she does when she wants her way.

What the hell do I do?

What the hell *can* I do?

I have no choice. I have to see her because she isn't going to go away.

"Give me five minutes and I'll save you from her."

"Thank you, Max."

Blair treats Mary poorly. Always has. And because Blair is Thomas's daughter, who is going to call her out for bad behavior?

Me. I should do it. Hell, I'm not going to be here

much longer anyway. The least I can do for Mary is make Blair show her some respect.

I hang up the phone and place my palms on my desk, lowering my head. "You aren't going to believe this shite."

"Your next client has arrived early."

"Aye, but that's not the kick in the bollocks. Blair is out there. She wants to see me between clients."

"Tell me you're joking."

"I wish."

"Dammit, she just never stops."

"At least you came in disguise. She won't recognize you as long as you don't make eye contact."

"I wasn't finished having my fun with you."

"We can pick up with this tonight, Miss Morata."

"I plan to."

Lou gets up from the couch and turns around to look. "Uh-oh. There's a wet spot on the cushion. Do you have something I could use to clean it up? And to clean me up?"

"Hold on a minute."

I go to the private toilet within my office and fetch a clean hand towel, tossing it to Lou.

"Dining room tables. Back seats. My office. Where do you think we'll do it next?"

"Hmm... let me think about it and I'll come up with something fun."

"You can make daily appointments with me if you like. A different name and disguise for each meeting."

"I have an even better idea. All of this shit with the Lochridges ends and you get a job somewhere else where I'm not a secret."

"You're right. That is a much better idea."

My wife goes into the bathroom as Lou and comes out as Miss Morata. "You look good as a platinum blonde."

"Are you suggesting that I bleach my hair?"

"No. I love your hair as is." I pick up a piece and twirl it around my finger. "The darker shades of brown with these wee streaks of honey are beautiful."

"Shades of brown and streaks of honey?" Lou giggles. "I don't know another man on earth who would say that about a woman's hair unless he was a hairdresser."

"I don't typically notice things like that, but I'm observant when it comes to you."

"What else have you observed about me?"

"That you've been in a good mood for the last couple of days." Unusually good.

"It's unusual for me to be in a good mood?"

"Let me rephrase. You're in an exceptionally good mood for a lass who will be starting her cycle soon."

"Are you saying that I'm irritable when it's time for my period?"

That's exactly what I'm saying but without saying it. "You can be a little moody sometimes."

"I'm sorry. I didn't realize."

"It's fine, mo maise. You don't have to apologize. You're entitled to being a little cranky."

Lou stands tall in her fuck-me pumps and smooths her dress. "As much as I hate it our time is up. Will Blair look at me and think I'm a rich client who wants you to invest my money?"

"She'll think you're a *beautiful* client."

"Even better." Lou kisses my mouth and then

wipes both of my lips with her thumb. "I'll see you at home around six?"

"Hopefully sooner. I'm going to try and sneak away around four thirty."

"Good. Ava Rose and I like it when you come home early."

"Me too." I like spending time with my girls.

Lou reaches up and touches the top of her wig. "Is it straight?"

"Looks grand."

"Don't spend too much time with the Blair Witch Project or I might become a jealous wife."

I chuckle. "Blair Witch Project?"

"Yeah. That's what I call her in my head."

"Fitting name but you should never be jealous of her. I despise that witch." I wink at Lou because I think I'm being clever by calling her a witch instead of a bitch.

"I know but I am somewhat jealous that she can waltz into this firm, insist on seeing you, and have her demand immediately met."

"Not much longer and we'll be rid of her." I say the words and I can see an immediate response forming in Lou's head. "Don't say it. I know, I know, I know we won't ever truly be rid of her because she's Ava Rose's family, but things will be better soon."

"I have a very strong feeling you're right. Things are going to be better sooner rather than later."

"You're certainly optimistic."

"No reason not to be."

Lou kisses her fingertips and blows a kiss in my direction. "Until tonight, Mr. Hutcheson."

I open the door for her and stand in the entrance,

watching her as she leaves. My two o'clock appointment, I presume, looks up from the book he's reading and scans my wife from head to toe as she walks by, paying close attention to her bum. And he isn't the only one.

Blair is watching me watch Lou and I'm caught. She sees me ogling my wife, and I don't mistake the jealousy or anger I see in her expression.

But I have zero fucks to give.

Blair walks by me and mutters something I can't decipher.

"You have five minutes. My next appointment arrived early and he's out there waiting."

"Who was that woman?"

I can't tell her Ina Morata. Blair is an intelligent woman. She could put together the pieces of Lou's clever alias. "Ana Morton."

"She looks very familiar."

No surprise there. She should.

"Perhaps she's in some of the same social circles as you?"

"No. I would remember her."

"True. She's quite an unforgettable woman."

"That's a rude thing to say to me."

"Is it?"

"We're engaged to be married. You aren't supposed to desire other women."

Fuck this shite. "Why are you here?"

"I came to tell you that I filed for divorce and Doug has moved out."

"We've already had this conversation. Filing means nothing. Your divorce could drag on for a long time."

"I know, but I wanted you to know that things are

moving, and Dad is going to see what he can do to expedite the process."

Thomas may have money and power but he can't change the law or the way its system works. Divorce takes as long as it takes. And thank fuck for that.

"All right. You've told me. Now I have a client to see."

Blair looks around my office and focuses on my couch. "The cushions on your sofa are out of place."

"So?"

"Has something happened in here?"

Fuck, it smells like sex in here?

"Do you mean something such as sitting on the furniture? Aye. I do that from time to time."

Blair goes to the sofa and straightens the cushions. "This kind of disarray doesn't appear professional to the clients of Lochridge. It looks like you just shagged on the sofa."

She runs her hand over the cushion and stills. "There's a wet spot on this one."

Fuck.

"I spilled my coffee earlier."

She lowers her face to the spot and sniffs like a fucking drug dog. "This doesn't smell like coffee."

"Maybe because I cleaned it up?"

"Did you fuck that woman? The blonde who was just in here?"

I'm so tempted to say yes. "I don't fuck clients. But if I did, it wouldn't be any of your business."

"That's where you're wrong, Max. You're engaged to marry me. That means you don't get to fuck anyone but me."

She's delusional.

"I'm not going to stand here and debate this with you while I have a client waiting to see me."

"I'll go, but I want you to tell me you understand what I'm saying about not fucking around with other people. I won't have it."

"I understand what you're saying." But understanding and abiding are two different things.

"Good. Because I will bury you so deep that you'll never see the light of day again if I find out you're unfaithful to me."

There it is. More talk of burying me.

I fear that Blair may be a bigger threat than I originally gave her credit for. And that's going to be a larger problem with Ava Rose's custody than I originally anticipated. I don't think I'm going to be able to deal with the Lochridges legally through the justice system.

I wanted to do this the right way. The honest way. For Ava Rose. And for Lou. I wanted to be the honorable man they deserve. But honorable intention will lose this fight. It's not an option.

I have only one choice. To fight dirtier than them.

It's time for a consultation with my Fellowship friends.

28

CAITRIONA HUTCHESON

DAMN, I'M LOOKING FORWARD TO THIS.

This spider has trapped her prey. Blair is caught in my web and doesn't even realize it yet. She's sitting in the back of our car right now believing that Hutch sent Calvin for her. But the icing on the cake? She also believes that Hutch is the one who will be waiting for her.

Wrong.

She's about to get the shock of her life.

Am I nervous? Maybe I was when I first arrived at the restaurant, but I'd say eager is a better word to describe how I feel after having two glasses of whisky. Can't lie. The amber liquid deposited a healthy dose of courage in my veins.

A little liquid courage never hurt anyone.

I spot Blair's ginger bob at the hostess stand, and I study her. Tight winter-white dress. Tall pumps. Not a hair out of place. She definitely came here with the intention of looking sexy for Hutch.

She's a beautiful woman. I can't deny that even though I'd like to.

I get up and move to the opposite seat so my back is to her when the hostess seats her at the table. I don't want her to see me and be tipped off about my presence, giving her the opportunity to make a run for it. Not that it would matter. A man named Sangster is waiting outside to grab her if she decides to not stick around to hear what I have to say.

There is a plan B in place and it isn't nearly as pleasant as plan A. She'll sit her skinny ass down at this table and hear me out if she knows what's good for her.

I turn and make eye contact with Blair when I hear the hostess say, "Your server will be with you in just a moment. Enjoy your dinner."

"Oh good. You made it." I gesture to the seat across from me. "Well, don't just stand there, silly. Sit down."

The hostess walks away, and my eyes bore into hers. "Sit, Blair. Now!"

Her jaw clenches and her nostrils flare. It looks like a different version of resting-bitch face from her usual one. And she looks as though she might be thinking of fleeing.

Better not, bitch. You won't like what awaits you outside.

She sits down and glares at me as though she believes a stare-down will intimidate me. It's incredibly satisfying to see how much she has underestimated me.

"You must be so disappointed to find yourself having dinner with *Mrs.* Hutcheson instead of Mr. Hutcheson."

"What are you talking about?"

I hold up my left hand. "I'm talking about this."

"You think a fake diamond on your left ring finger is going to convince me that Max married you?"

"I don't think my ring will convince you of anything. That's why I brought this."

I open up what I'm calling the Blair's-bad-behavior binder—the folder containing all of the filth I have on her—and I remove a photograph that was taken of Hutch and me while we said our vows.

"Our wedding was beautiful. Very quaint. Very... *private.*"

My nemesis stares at the picture, saying nothing. She clears her throat, forcing a faux cough.

"Don't you think my wedding gown was stunning? Hutch told me I looked like a regal queen. And that's what he treated me like on our wedding night. The consummation was wow—just wow. I've never experienced anything like that."

"I warned you. And I warned Max about what would happen if you came back into his life." Blair holds up our wedding photo and rips it down the middle into two halves. "This is only a small demonstration of how I'll tear the two of you apart. Your marriage won't last long enough for him to bring you roses on your one-month anniversary."

"Too late. He brought me a dozen. They were pink, in case you're wondering." I giggle. "Pink roses have a special meaning for us. But you probably already know what they mean, considering how much you know about my time at Inamorata."

She looks away, shaking her head, and I enjoy the confusion I see etched on her face in the lines on her forehead and around her eyes. I try to imagine what this moment must feel like for her. How she must be trying to sort out in her head how she could have been so stupid. So fooled by both of us.

"Caitriona Hutcheson. It's a strong Scottish name, don't you think?"

"You should gloat while you can, but let's be clear about it. It'll be short-lived."

"Go ahead. Tell me how Hutch will no longer have a job at Lochridge. Tell me how no one in Edinburgh is going to hire a man who married a *prostitute*. Tell me how humiliated I'll be when everyone finds out about my former profession. And tell me how I should consider Ava Rose a soon-to-be-distant memory because your family will never let me be in her life."

"I don't have to say it when you just said everything for me."

"Nothing you'd like to add to the list?"

"I think you covered it all. To add anything else on top of that would just be cruel."

I chuckle and she looks at me as though I've lost my mind. And it's in that moment that I realize she's serious. She really doesn't see what a cruel individual she is.

I pick up one of the binders and place it on the table in front of her. "We should get on with this because I have a husband waiting for me at home."

"What is this supposed to be?"

"Open to page one and I'll introduce you to Blair's-bad-behavior binder."

"You are such a waste of my time."

"Well, you're a waste of oxygen. Trust me when I say that I'm happy to skip the courtesy of going over the file with you. Nothing would please me more than to pass along copies to your parents, your sisters, and Doug if that's how you'd like to play this game. His divorce attorney would have a field day with the shit in this binder."

She sighs and opens the folder. "Numbers and dashes. I don't know what the hell this is supposed to be."

"I have friends. Friends you don't know about. Friends who want to help me and this is how they did it."

"This is how they did what?"

"Hacked your computer. Hacked your email. Hacked your phone and the messages you've received and sent."

Her eyes widen. "Whaaat? You can't do that."

"No, I certainly can't but my friends can." I reach over and place my finger on page one of her folder. "This number is your IP address. Yours. No one else's. And you were too dumb to change it to a hidden IP address so everything in this folder came from you. Thank you for being stupid and making this so easy for us."

She pushes my hand away and glares at page one, softly muttering one profanity and then another.

"If you'll turn to page two…."

She does as I say and I'd almost swear that I can see the color draining from her face.

"Those are the text messages between you and Mina where you are encouraging her to sign up for a profile on a singles website. You even sent her a link to the one where she'd be able to meet affluential men. And that's what she eventually did, which was only the beginning of your plan."

I reach over and turn the page for her. "Page six is where things really begin to get interesting—and disturbing—because these are pages and pages and pages of messages that were exchanged between Mina and her lover, Roman Kirk. But it wasn't he who was sending these romantic and often kinky messages to her. It was you."

Blair flips through the binder, scanning each page.

"You were catphishing your own sister with a phony profile. What kind of person does something like that?"

Although I've seen the proof and know it to be the truth, I almost want her to deny it. I don't know why but I want her to try to convince me she's a better person than this. Because there's something so damn discouraging about knowing that there are people like her in the world, people who care so little about hurting others.

"You established an online romance between Mina and an imaginary lover and then paid a complete stranger, the man you used for creating the fake profile, to go out with her and form a fake relationship. You paid him to have sex with your sister. You paid him to make her believe he loved her. And you didn't do it because you thought it would make her happy. You did it because you wanted her husband for yourself."

She's silent, staring at the binder.

"You don't have anything to say about what you did to your sister?"

"What do you want me to say? You already know everything that happened."

"Your sister made a baby with this man. She loved him and everything between them was a lie you created. Don't you feel any kind of remorse for that?"

Nothing. No response.

"Mina told him she was pregnant and he confessed everything to her. She knew what you did."

"Who told you that?"

"Roman Kirk."

"I don't believe you."

"I recorded my meeting with him. I can send you a copy if you'd like to watch it. Or I can email it to Thomas, Lundy, Beth, Elsie, and Doug and you can have family movie night. I'm sure they'd love to discuss it with you."

"I paid him to stay quiet," she whispers, I think maybe telling herself.

"You think your chump change was enough to keep him quiet when I waved big money in front of him? Honey, you should have worked out some kind of contingency plan if you wanted him to keep his mouth shut."

"What did he tell Mina?"

"Everything. She knew what you'd done to her."

For the first time, I think I see some kind of remorse on her face. "Oh my God."

"She was devastated when she left Roman's flat that night. That was the same night that she got into the accident that killed her. Her last thoughts before she died were of the way you betrayed her."

Blair places her hands over her ears. "Stop."

"She was devastated and distracted as she drove."

She shakes her head violently. "Don't say it."

"Some people might make the claim that ultimately you are the reason she was distracted that night. The reason she had the accident. The reason she died. And they wouldn't be wrong."

"Stop, please. I can't take this."

"What you've done is vile and unforgivable. I wonder what your mum and dad would say if they knew what you did to their daughter. What would your sisters say?"

"You can't tell them. They would hate me. My dad would disown me."

And there it is—the desperation I needed and wanted to see in Blair. She's tangled in my web.

"You stand to lose everything if I show this binder to your family and husband. I'm going to need you to convince me why I should keep all of these vile secrets to myself."

"I will give you a hundred thousand pounds."

She thinks she can buy my silence with money? "Don't insult me."

"What do you want?"

"You'll stop using Ava Rose's paternity as leverage against Hutch and me. No more threats. No more blackmail."

"I won't tell anyone about Ava Rose's paternity if you keep my secret."

"Damn right you won't tell anyone, but that isn't all I want from you. You're going to convince your family that Hutch and I belong together. You're going to do whatever it takes to make your father allow him to leave the firm on good terms. And you're going to convince them that I am a wonderful stepmother for Ava Rose. So wonderful that my adopting her as my daughter would be a wonderful and healthy thing for her."

"Do you have any idea what you're asking of me?"

"I certainly do and I don't give a damn how you make it happen as long as it happens."

She stares at me blankly, saying nothing.

My head moves up and down. "Nod and tell me you understand and will fulfill my demands or this binder of bad behavior will land on your father's desk first thing in the morning."

"I understand and I'll make it happen," she says through clenched teeth.

"Agree to all of my terms."

"I agree to all of your terms."

"Tell anyone about Ava Rose's paternity or show up at our house unannounced again and *I* will bury *you* in a mountain of shit so deep you'll never see the light of day again." I lean closer and lower my voice. "You think you know me and what I'm about, but you don't. You have no idea what I'm capable of, princess. Fuck with me again and you'll find yourself in a very small rectangular dirt room. Do we have an understanding?"

"Yes."

"Never contact Roman Kirk again. He has no idea that Ava Rose exists. If that changes, I'll know it was you who told him. To drag that man into her life would be a terrible disservice to her."

"We agree on that much."

"We better agree on more than that."

"This must be very satisfying for you."

"Honey, the real satisfaction is waiting at home for me." I get up and toss the other binder in front of her. "Please know that if anything should happen to me, I have multiple copies of these and the video.

Both are in place to be sent to your family and the authorities."

I pick up my whisky and toss back the last of it. "Calvin is my driver so find your own fucking way home."

29

MAXWELL HUTCHESON

BRADY LEANS CLOSE TO ME AND LOWERS HIS VOICE. "Your wife just walked in."

What? Did he just say that my wife is here? "Come again, mate?"

"Cait. She just walked into this bar."

It's late. Why is she here instead of home?

I'm at this bar tonight to watch the Super Bowl with my Lochridge colleagues. She knows this, so something must have happened. I can't think of another reason that she'd come here.

I twist on my barstool and look at the entrance, my eyes meeting Lou's. When she smiles, I see that all is well and my fears instantly melt away.

"Dammmn. Would you look at what just walked in here?" one of my colleagues says as Lou walks past us, his eyes glued to her bum. "That is one fit lass."

She walks past me to the hallway where the toilets are, and I interpret that as my cue to follow.

"She didn't randomly show up here. I need to see what's going on."

Brady reaches over and grabs my beer, claiming it as his own. "You'll probably be a while. I'll take care of this for you."

"Fine but you're buying the next round."

"I have a feeling you won't be back for another round."

Lou looks so happy that even her eyes are smiling when I approach her in the hallway. "What are you doing here?"

"I'm sorry to show up like this. I knew you wouldn't be home until very late, and I'm too excited to wait because something wonderful has happened."

Is she pregnant?

I don't think so. She would consider that kind of news to be too special to share with me while standing beside a sports bar loo.

Ned, one of the newer financial advisors, approaches the toilets and lifts a brow when he notices Lou. "Hello."

"Hi," Lou says.

The loo door closes and I whisper, "We can't be seen together like this by Lochridge employees. Too many eyes and ears. Meet me behind the building in five minutes."

Her smile widens. "Okay."

I return to my seat and reclaim my beer. "I'll take that back from you, thank you very much."

"What does the wifey want?" Brady's voice is low.

"I don't know yet. We're meeting out back in five minutes."

"Must be important for her to come here when she knows you're surrounded by half of the Lochridge firm."

"I'm certain it must be."

"Good news, I hope."

"I believe it is. She used the word wonderful to describe it."

I finish off what's left of my beer and casually exit the bar, finding Lou right where I told her to be. "What is it, love?"

She reaches out and cradles my face, coming up on her tiptoes to place a kiss against my lips. "Listen to me with an open mind. Don't jump to conclusions before I finish. Can you do that?"

"Aye."

"As you know, I've been spending time with Bleu and the other wives."

"I'm aware." And I'm pleased by the way the wives have been so welcoming to Lou. Rachel is a loyal friend, but she's busy with Claud. Lou needs other friends.

"You told me I couldn't ask who or what the Breckenridges are, and I've honored that, but I have suspicions. And I knew that if I was right, they could help me—help us—and so I asked."

"You asked for what? And who did you ask?"

"I asked Bleu for help with our Blair problem."

"Oh, Lou. I wish you hadn't done that." She doesn't understand what they are.

"You promised to not jump to conclusions. Remember?"

"Aye, I know."

"Bleu and Shaw, well actually Shaw's contact, hacked into Blair's computer and phone."

"Oh fuck."

"We discovered awful things, Hutch. The things that she's done are so much worse than either of us could have imagined."

Astonished, I listen as Lou describes Mina's gullibility and Blair's betrayal. And although I know both women well, it's difficult to believe that Mina would be so easily exploited and Blair so vile.

I'm sad for Mina. Even she didn't deserve to be treated that way, especially in the last moments of her life. She must have been so hurt.

"What do we do with this information?"

"Nothing. I've already handled Blair."

"You've handled her?"

"I turned the tables on that bitch. There'll be no more threats. No more blackmail. Ava Rose belongs to us, and our marriage doesn't have to be a secret anymore. The nightmare is over."

"It's really over?"

"It's really over."

The timing... it's almost as if she knew what I was contemplating and saved me from going through with it.

I wrap my arms around Lou and pick her up, spinning her around in the air. "I am married to the most amazing woman in the world."

I return her feet to the ground and cradle her face in my hands. "Let's go home, mo maise."

"What about the Super Bowl?"

"Forget the Super Bowl."

Ava Rose is already asleep when we arrive home, but Lou and I go to the nursery and stand beside the crib looking at her. "She's ours."

"Yes, she is."

"What do you think Mina would say about my being Ava Rose's mother?"

"I think she would be happy that her daughter has you as her mum."

"I obviously didn't know Mina, but I think she'd choose me over Blair."

"Knowing what we know now, I'm certain that is the truth."

I wrap my arms around Lou from behind and kiss the side of her neck. "I'm ready to try for another one whenever you're ready."

Lou twists and looks at me over her shoulder. "Are you talking about what I think you're talking about?"

"She turns one this month. If you got pregnant in a few months, they'd be two years apart. Isn't that what we said we wanted?"

"That's what we said."

"Then stop your birth control and we'll start trying in May."

Lou turns and wraps her arms around my shoulders. "I think we should practice making a baby before trying the real thing. You know, just to be sure we know what we're doing."

"I think that is an excellent idea."

She places a quick kiss against my mouth and tugs on my hand. "Come on. I'm going to give you your very own halftime show."

Fuck yeah. "I like the sound of that."

Once we're in our bedroom, Lou places her hands on my hips and walks backward, pulling me toward the bed. She sits and glides to the center. Lifting her foot, she curls her toes around the waistband of my jeans. "Take 'em off. Take everything off."

"Yes, ma'am."

My jeans and Y-fronts drop to the floor and she moves to the edge of the bed. At first, I think she's going to stand and undress but instead she moves to her all fours and reaches into the drawer on the nightstand.

Condoms? She wants to use condoms? Why? We just agreed that we both wanted to try for a baby soon. "There aren't any in there."

Lou laughs. "I'm not looking for condoms, goofball."

She smiles and sits back on her haunches, holding up my wedding band. "This is what I'm looking for."

She reaches for my left hand, slides my wedding band on my finger, and kisses the top. "You can wear this for everyone to see now."

"And I will, mo maise. With pride." Because I am proud to be her husband.

I wrap my arms around her and press my mouth to hers, tongue gliding against tongue. I think I could devour her here and now.

I grip the front of her dress. "Take it off. Take all of it off."

"Yes, Mr. Hutcheson."

Lou grips the bottom of her dress and tugs it upward, pulling it over her head and dropping it on the floor. The bra and knickers go next and she's bare, except for the ring on her left hand.

She slides to the center of the bed and lies on her back. Using her index finger, she beckons me. "Come here, husband. It's time to practice making a baby."

Crawling up her body, I take my time, leaving a path of kisses up her belly and chest. When we're face-to-face, she grasps the back of my neck and pulls me down, bringing our mouths together.

Tongue against tongue, my mouth makes love to hers. Slow. Deep. Loving. But possessive. Always possessive. Because this woman is mine.

"I love you, Caitriona Hutcheson."

Her hazel eyes stare at my blue as I hover above her. "And I love you, Maxwell Hutcheson. I love our family. I love our life."

Her legs part and I nestle my body between them until my hard cock is against her warm, inviting entrance. "We get to do this for fun for a while longer, but it'll soon have a special purpose behind it."

"I know. It scares me but in a good way." Her body trembles as she says the words.

"I feel the exact same way, mo maise."

My cock is pressed against her, ready to enter. All it will take is one thrust and I'll glide inside her slick canal. But I don't get the chance. She impatiently lifts her hips, forcing my tip to slide into her entrance. "Eager much?"

"You know I'm always eager."

That's one thing I can say about my wife. She has never been guilty of lying beneath me, praying for sex to hurry and be over. "You're never at a loss for enthusiasm."

Her ankles dig into my arse, forcing me deeper inside of her. "I want it. Give it to me."

"I'm going to give it to you."

Reaching behind her, I wrap my hand around her lower back. Lifting her hips off the bed, I sink into her as far as possible before pulling back and doing it again.

I place my free hand over her lower belly. Right there beneath my palm is where our child will grow. And it will soon if things go well.

And what if things don't go well? What if Lou's previous pregnancy was some kind of flukish miracle and I actually do have an issue with sterility?

I can't think about that right now.

Her legs are bent on each side of my hips and I grasp them, pushing back. Opening her up to take more of me.

I slip my hand between our bodies and feel for that point where we connect. No beginning. No end. So close it's as though we're one being.

I find that spot—the one that drives her crazy every time I touch it—and I stroke the tight nub with my fingertips. Her breath quickens and she grasps my back, pulling me against her tighter, grinding her hips against me.

"That's it. Just like that," she says in that breathy voice I love so much.

She grinds harder and I know what comes next. She does.

Her inner walls squeeze around my cock, contracting in rhythm. Once. Twice. And then again and again until I lose count because I'm lost in my own world coming apart.

Exploding.

Flowing.

Spilling inside her.

I push her legs back and apart, thrusting deeply one last time, and holding steady. This is how I'll do it when we actually try.

I lower my upper body and hover above her, my elbows pressing into the mattress on each side of her head. I pepper kisses across her forehead, nose, cheeks, and finally her mouth—her mouth that is now grinning. "What is it?"

"I'm amazed by the changes in you. You've done a complete one-eighty."

"That's what happens when you meet the right woman."

Mina wasn't the woman for me. It may sound crazy but I almost feel as though my failed marriage has played a hand in preparing me to be the best husband I can be for Lou.

"I'm no fool. I know a good thing when I see it. And from the moment I laid eyes on you, I knew there would be something special between us." I remember telling Brady I wanted to feel a connection when I saw the right inamorata. And I did.

She smiles. "I didn't know what it was, but I felt something too."

"I never imagined myself loving a woman the way I love you. And I damn sure never imagined myself wanting to have children."

She strokes the sides of my face. "I hope they have your eyes."

"Two can have my eyes and two can have yours. But I want all of them to have these adorable little freckles scattered across their noses."

"I want them to be tall like you. Being short sucks."

"Short happens to look very cute on you."

"I can assure you it's only cute to those who aren't short."

I kiss her and pull out slowly. "If we were trying to get pregnant tonight, would you want me to pull out or leave my cock in for a while like a stopper to prevent my sperm from leaking out?"

She laughs. "I haven't given it that much thought, but I see you have."

"Aye, I've been thinking about it for a while."

"You haven't said much about it."

"There was really no point in talking about it until our lives were on a steady course." I've allowed the Lochridges to dictate so much in my life. But those days are over. "I'm giving notice in the morning."

"That makes me so happy."

"I don't know what I'll do for a job yet, but I'll figure out something." Maybe start my own firm. I've always wanted that.

"Nothing is holding us to Edinburgh."

"Are you thinking we should make the move to Glasgow?"

"I am. One hundred percent. Wouldn't it be wonderful for Ava Rose and our other children to grow up near your family?"

"They're *our* family. You're a Hutcheson now. And yes. I would love for our children to grow up near our family."

"I've never had a real family, and I want that in my life on a daily basis. I don't want to be closer to them just for our children. I want it for me too."

If Lou wants to be near the family, then I want to give her that. "I think that's what we should do. And I think we should begin working on that very soon."

"We can't move before the semester ends. I'm so close to being finished."

"We'll stay long enough for you to graduate. That'll give me time to finish tying up loose ends with my clients. And it'll give us time to find a new house."

"Do you think any of your clients will want to leave Lochridge and come with you?"

A lot of them don't care for Thomas. "Possibly although I would never encourage that. It would be entirely up to them."

"I'm not worried. There'll be plenty of clients in Glasgow. And if there aren't, it's okay. I don't need wealth to be happy. All I need is you and our family."

"You never have to worry about money, Lou. I have enough funds invested and put away to sustain us comfortably for the duration of our lives and our children's lives."

"I figured as much."

"I know how strong and independent you are, but with me your fight is over. I've got you, mo maise. I want to take care of you. And I want you to take care of me and our family."

"We do take care of each other, don't we?"

"We absolutely do."

Lou is my partner in life. My love. My everything.

I walked into that Inamorata gala seeking a sexy female companion for the summer. Instead, I got a beautiful wife for a lifetime. A loving mother for my daughter. A woman who opened my heart to the child that I didn't know I could ever want and love.

She is my beautiful ever after.

30

CAITRIONA HUTCHESON

IT'S OFFICIAL. I'M A GRADUATE OF THE UNIVERSITY OF Edinburgh. I have earned my degree in English language and literature.

Gus and Clarissa. Sara, Adam, and the boys. Ian, Shannon, and Pearl. Rachel and Claud. And my heart —my Hutch and Ava Rose. Everyone I love is surrounding me at this restaurant tonight to celebrate my accomplishment. And it feels amazing. I thought I might never have people like these in my life.

While it's incredibly satisfying to know that I have finally accomplished what I set out to do, I find that it is my life with Hutch and Ava Rose that brings me the most joy and satisfaction.

Everyone has a calling in life. I can't say what mine will be five or ten years from now but today, my number-one calling is to be a wife and mother. That's where my heart is. It's where my loyalty lies.

The writing will come when it comes.

Hutch reaches for my hand, bringing it to his lips.

"My wife, the graduate. You did it, mo maise. I'm so proud of you."

"I think I'm proudest because being finished means that we can finally move to the new house in Glasgow." School has been delaying the start of the rest of our lives for too long.

Hutch and I bought a house on thirty acres near his parents' home on the golf course. He insisted that we have plenty of acreage to build a barn and bring the horses. Sol, Prissy, and Nevan are our family too.

"I'm excited about our new lives in Glasgow."

"I am too."

Gus stands and clinks his wine glass with his knife. "A toast to my bonnie daughter-in-law." Everyone around the table quietens and Gus continues, "We're so proud of your accomplishment today but even prouder of the wife you are to Max and the mother you are to Ava Rose. We love you dearly."

"What a lovely thing to say. Thank you."

Murmurs of love and congratulations come from around the table, the words overlapping at once, and tears pool in my lower lids. Because these people love me.

They're happy for me. Proud of me. Want the best for me.

And I've never had that in my life.

It's an amazing feeling. Everyone should feel this way at some point of their life.

Dinner is exceptional as it always is at this restaurant. It never disappoints.

I sit back, placing my hand over my lower stomach. "I ate too much."

Hutch leans close and lowers his voice. "No

worries. I have some vigorous baby-making exercise planned for you when we get home."

"You do, huh?"

"Indeed, I do, Mrs. Hutcheson. I've been reading up on the best positions. They look like a lot of fun."

"You've been doing research, huh?"

"A wee bit."

"I'm excited to see what you've come up with."

"Are you ready to go so I can show you?"

"I'm ready if you are."

Clarissa and I make a visit to the loo on the way out, and I'm sitting on the toilet when someone tries to open the door from the outside. "Sorry, occupied."

I rush to finish my business but go still when I hear the women on the other side of the stall talking.

"I just saw Maxwell Hutcheson out there. Is that his new wife?"

"You saw Max?"

Shit. I think that's Blair's voice.

I might wonder what the odds were of running into her here, but it wouldn't be unusual for her to frequent a restaurant like this one. It's damn fancy.

"He's sitting with ten, maybe twelve people out there. The woman beside him has long brown hair. Short. Petite. Very pretty."

"That sounds like his nasty bitch wife who won't let us see Ava Rose anymore."

It's true. She doesn't see Ava Rose anymore but not because I've had anything to do with it. Blair is the reason that Blair no longer sees her niece. She lost all interest in Ava Rose once she found out that Hutch wasn't going to marry her.

I'm pretty sure the rest of the family is on their way to losing interest in her as well. They rarely call to check on her and never ask for visits anymore. It's been at least a month since we've heard from them.

With the Lochridges, she was like a new toy who has now lost her shine. Hutch says that's how all of them are with everything in their lives except money and power. Nothing holds their attention for long before they're on to the next most exciting thing. And that's more than okay with us. That little girl has all the love she needs in us. She'll never know their toxicity. They're doing her a favor by choosing to not be in her life.

"I don't know where Max went slumming to find such an uncouth American. She's certainly not Lochridge calibre. But I guess it's fitting, considering the kind of family he comes from. He has a more similar background with this wife than he ever did with Mina."

"I can't believe she won't let you see Mina's daughter. She's your own flesh and blood. That's wrong. You should do something about that."

"One hundred percent. You should take legal action, Blair. You know you'd win. Who wouldn't rule in your favor?"

The trio of women go silent and all smiles fade when I open the stall door. "Pardon me. The nasty bitch wife needs to wash her hands."

I will not stoop to her level.

I will not stoop to her level.

I will not stoop to her level.

Clarissa opens the other stall door, and I realize that in my anger I'd forgotten she was in here. And then another realization hits me when I see the expression on her face: she heard Blair insult the Hutchesons.

I can take being insulted. I'm accustomed to it, but no one gets to insult Clarissa and her family. "You can say what you like about me but not Clarissa and her family. Apologize."

Blair looks at me and smiles. "I don't apologize for speaking the truth."

"Apologize. Now."

"No."

I count to three in my mind. Slowly. "I care what my mother-in-law thinks of me, and that's the only reason I'm not going to knock the hell out of you right now."

"Go ahead. Knock the hell out of her. I'll think even more of you if you do." Clarissa steps between the two friends and me. "I can take care of these two if they try to be heroes."

I may be small, but I'm fast. And my fist collides with Blair's nose before she has time to think about retreating. The stream of blood immediately trickling down her upper lip is satisfying.

"Holy shite. There goes that rhinoplasty," one of the girls says.

"You may be wee, but you are mighty," Clarissa says.

Blair reaches up and touches her face. "You broke my nose?"

"I certainly hope so. Maybe then you'll think twice before looking down it at other people."

Clarissa and I leave the loo, and I bring my hand up to inspect my wedding ring.

"Good job, lass. That was a mighty fine left hook. Where did you learn to do that?"

"My friend Bleu taught me." I open and close my

fist. And it hurts like a mutha. "I may have just broken my hand. I hit her harder than I intended."

"Well, you didn't hit her harder than *I* intended. She deserved that plus so much more." Clarissa reaches for my hand and inspects it. "You should take off your wedding rings before your fingers swell."

My entire hand is throbbing and already feeling tight. "That's a good idea. I'd hate to have to cut them off."

Ava Rose holds out her arms for me, but my hand is throbbing so badly. "Let Da hold you, baby."

"What's wrong?"

"I'll tell you on the way home."

Calvin has barely pulled away from the curb when Hutch revisits the conversation about what is going on.

"Blair and her friends came into the loo. They didn't know we were in there, and Blair said nasty things about me and your family."

"Did she upset my mum?"

"I wouldn't say upset. Pissed off would be a better way to describe what your mom was."

"My mum can get aff her heid if someone talks shite about the family. She's not okay with that."

"I told Blair that I cared about what Clarissa thought of me and that she was the only reason I wasn't going to knock the hell out of her. Your mom told me to go for it. So I did."

"Wait… what?"

"Your mom wanted me to punch Blair so I did. I think I broke her nose." I hold up my fist. "And maybe my hand."

"You brawled in the loo at the restaurant?"

"Yes, and it was great. I've been wanting to do that for a while."

"Wow. My wife is a brawler. I had no idea." He reaches over Ava Rose's car seat and caresses the back of my neck. "That's hot."

"You're not embarrassed that I acted so unrefined?"

"You defended our family. I couldn't be prouder of you, Lou." Hutch lowers his voice. "And I also couldn't be more turned on."

"That's good because I believe we have some baby-making to do," I whisper.

"Aye, we do."

I stopped my birth control three months ago in preparation for what we're calling the next chapter of our lives. Tonight is our first try, and while it's the same act we've engaged in I don't know how many times before, everything about this time is different.

Hutch leans forward to look at Ava Rose in her seat. "I hope she doesn't wake and try to stay up when we move her from the seat to her crib."

She does that sometimes. Well, a lot of times. "I hope she doesn't cry to stay in our bed."

"Fuck, I didn't even think about that."

We spoiled Ava Rose by letting her sleep with us for so long. Convincing her to sleep in her crib in her new nursery has been trying at times.

"It's been a long day for her."

"It's been a long day for all of us." And a stressful one. I'm glad graduation is behind me.

"Are you too tired to try tonight?"

"No. I want to. But I may fall asleep right after though."

"After won't hurt my pride, but I don't think I could take your going to sleep in the middle."

I giggle. "Then you should do your best to make sure I stay awake."

"Oh, you're on."

After we're home, I go to our bedroom and prepare myself for our first baby-making session while Hutch gets Ava Rose down in her crib for the night. I know things must have gone well when I come out of the bathroom and see him sitting on the side of the bed, wearing only a pair of boxer briefs.

I stop in the doorway and lean against the frame. Shifting my weight to one leg, I put my hand on my hip.

Black baby-doll top split up the middle, barely covering my breasts. Exposed belly. Tiny black triangle between my legs. Fuck-me-now facial expression.

It's the ultimate prelude to baby-making.

"What does Da think?"

"Da loves."

Walking toward him, I realize that every step brings us closer to making this actually happen. And I'm overcome by the love I feel for this man when I think about what we're doing tonight.

He stands when I reach him and I dip my fingers into the waistband of his underwear, pushing them down his thighs. He kicks out of the fabric and I feel his full, thick cock against my stomach when he pulls me close.

We clumsily turn, our mouths not separating until I sit on the bed and glide to the middle. Using my index finger, I use it to coax him closer. "Get up here and put a baby inside me."

"Yes, ma'am."

Taking his time, he crawls up my body as he leaves a path of kisses beginning at my belly. When we're face-to-face, I grasp the back of his neck. "Kiss me."

I pull him down so our mouths meet and his makes love to mine. Slowly. Deeply. Lovingly.

When we stop kissing, he pulls away and looks at my face. "Tonight could change everything."

He stares into my eyes as he hovers above, and I run my fingertips down the bridge of his nose. "I hope so."

He kisses the side of my face and moves his mouth down the length of my neck before unfastening the ribbon that holds my top together. But before he does, he places a kiss between my breasts. And a thought strikes me. If we conceive tonight, it'll only be a matter of months before I put a newborn to these breasts for nursing. I look forward to that.

Hutch unfastens my top and pulls the straps down, leaving me topless. Next, he hooks his fingers into my waistband and drags my panties down my legs.

Face-to-face.

Bare skin to bare skin.

Heart to heart.

Open invitation.

He nestles his body between my parted legs until his hard cock presses against me. As always, a slick opening greets him. When I lift my hips, the crown pushes just inside me and then glides all the way in with ease.

"I love how you're always wet for me."

It's true. All Hutch has to do is look at me and my

body reacts. I'm sensitive to him. I get dripping wet for the man because he has conquered me. Broke through my walls. He's the only man who's ever been strong enough to do so, and I adore him for it.

He is my world. My everything.

He thrusts himself inside me until the base of his cock hits my entrance. Buried to the hilt. He closes his eyes and holds that position for a brief moment before rocking in and out of me slowly.

His pace gradually quickens but not to a point of aggression. Not even close. This is making love. And hopefully making a baby.

I cup the back of his neck with my hands and pull his face to mine. "I love you so much."

He stretches upward and presses a kiss to my forehead. "I love you too, mo maise."

Closed eyes. The muscles in his face and neck flexed. "I'm going to come."

I hear those words and I wrap my arms and legs around him, squeezing. I hold him tightly and he remains unmoving inside of me, his body filling mine with a part of himself that will join with a part of me and make our baby.

Maybe.

With his forehead still pressed to mine, his weight covers me like a blanket. He remains inside of me, and the only movement happening between us is the rise and fall of our lungs.

"Did we really just do that?"

"Aye. We really just did that." He lowers his mouth to mine, lightly kissing my lips. "And now you need to lie on your back with your hips elevated."

"Elevated how?"

"The article said we could use a pillow, but I have something else in mind."

He rises and kneels between my legs, patting the tops of his thighs. "Put your bum here and your ankles on my shoulders."

I lift my hips from the bed and he shoves a pillow under my butt before grabbing my feet and putting them on his shoulders. "You're turning me upside down?"

"That's the gist, I guess."

"You really want this to work, don't you?"

I've been surprised by his interest in researching natural ways to increase the odds.

"You know me, Lou. I'm astute in everything I do."

"Do you really think this position helps?" We didn't do it before and I seem to have gotten pregnant easily.

"I don't know how much it helps, but it certainly doesn't hurt."

"Do you have any other fun positions for us to try?"

"A whole list of them. Missionary was just to get warmed up. We're trying the plow next."

"The plow?" I giggle because it sounds so silly. "Explain that one, please."

"Picture me holding a farmer's plow. Your legs are the handles. Your arms and head are the chisel part on the ground. I'm going to stand and you're going to put your head and arms on the bed."

"I'm facedown on the bed with my ass and legs in the air?" That's just great.

"Fuck yeah."

"Well, that'll be the first time we've done it like that."

"And I strongly suspect it won't be the last time."

"You think you're going to enjoy plowing my fields, huh?"

"Aye, and when I'm done cultivating your land, I'm going to plant my seed."

"My, my. You are a clever one tonight, Mr. Hutcheson."

He smiles and I wait for more clever words but they don't come.

"What is it?"

"I'm remembering all the times when I thought you were your most beautiful."

"Go on. I need to hear some flattery because I don't feel very beautiful like this."

"The night we met at the Inamorata gala. The first time you lay beneath me. When you told me you loved me the first time. When I saw how much you love Ava Rose. When you became my wife. And even though you might not think so, right now." He turns his head and kisses the side of my ankle. "In this moment you are so damn beautiful to me."

I reach out and run my fingers through the bristly hairs on his thighs. "Hutch?"

"What is it, mo maise?"

"I think you should plow my field now."

"You do, huh?"

"Yes. Right now."

And that's exactly what he does.

31

MAXWELL HUTCHESON

IT'S OUR LAST WEEKEND IN EDINBURGH. CAN'T SAY I'M sorry about that. I'm looking forward to moving into our new house in Glasgow.

But I am going to miss this fucking dobber. He's been my best mate since I went to work at Lochridge.

"Lou really likes Ella. Maybe the two of you can come up for the weekend after we're settled into the new house."

"Aye. I know Ella would like that. She enjoys spending time with you two since you're our hash-tag-couple-goals."

"How is that going by the way? Your extended relationship?"

"It's good." Brady chuckles. "It's great actually."

"Cora chose well?"

"She did. But she should have for what it cost."

"Worth every pound though, aye?"

"One hundred percent worth it. Ella is everything I've ever wanted."

"Are you in love with her?"

"Let's just say I can see the potential."

"Is she the kind of lass you'd want to marry?"

"Possibly."

"Good. I'm happy things are going well for you." Brady is a good man. He deserves to be happy.

"What about your brother and his nuptials? That'll be here before you know it."

"Only a month away."

"Is he ready for that and everything it includes?"

"I think he is. He's grown up a lot since Pearl was born." A child does that to you.

"Having a child changed you."

"With me, I think it was the wife more than the child."

"True. Lou has changed you but in a good way."

I think it's time to drop the bomb on Brady. "We're trying to have a baby."

"Well. Fuck. Me."

"Sorry, mate. Can't. I have to save all of my spunk for Lou."

"Hey, Cameron, are you going to pour my beers or do I have to come around there and do it myself?" the barmaid shouts.

"Calm your tits, Maggie. I'll get to them in a minute."

Cameron. Bartender.

Lou's Cameron?

Fuck, it pisses me off that I called him that in my head just now.

Cameron Stewart is Lou's past. She's my wife. We have a family. We're trying to have another baby. A man from her past means nothing.

Except it's bugging me. I want to know if this bartender is Cameron Stewart. I want to know if this is the man who tried to win Lou back while we were apart. The man who proclaimed his love for my wife.

A husband just needs to know shite like that.

And he needs to claim what is his so a fucker like Cameron Stewart doesn't come around trying to fuck with his wife.

"Let's move to the bar."

"No fucking way. I have a perfect view of the game from here. I won't be able to see it from over there."

"Just do this for me, please."

"I might if you tell me why."

"This bartender. I think he's Lou's ex."

"Why do you care even if he is? He's part of Cait's past."

"I need to set some shite straight with him if he's her ex."

"O-fucking-kay." Brady stands and shoves his chair under the table. "Jealous possessive alpha motherfucker."

"That's accurate."

We move to the bar and he washes a few glasses before noticing us. "What can I get you?"

"Tomatin."

"For you too, mate?"

"Aye."

"Tomatin's a nice choice. Smooth."

He grabs two glasses, pouring each two fingers high, and I push a bill across the counter when he tells me the total. "I've got this round."

"You've got all of them for making me leave my good seat."

"Fair enough. Drinks on me tonight."

I study the bartender trying to decide if he looks

like the guy in the photo I saw on Lou's phone, and I can't decide. It's been too long since I saw it.

Fuck this.

"Hey, mate. Seems like you've served me drinks somewhere else before."

"I worked at The Last Drop for a few years."

I fucking knew it.

"You worked with Cait and Rachel?"

"Oh yeah. I know those lasses well. I haven't seen Rachel since she stopped working at the pub, but I ran into Cait on the train a while back." He leans closer. "And between me and you, she's a mighty fine shag. I plan on getting some more of that next time I run into her."

"Ohhh fuck," Brady says and gets up. "I'm going to the toilet."

"She is an excellent shag. And I should know. Because she's my wife."

"Your wife?"

"Listen and listen well because you'll only get one warning. Cait is mine. If you try to talk to her again, I will kill you. If you ever see her out and you tell her you love her, I will kill you. If you ever touch her, I will kill you. Zero hesitation."

Cameron holds up his hands. "I had no idea she was married. Honest-to-God truth."

"You should consider yourself lucky I haven't come across this bar and choked the fuck out of you for talking about my wife like that."

"My apologies. I didn't know."

"Well, you know now."

Aye, a bigger man might have walked out of here without saying a word to Cameron Stewart, but I couldn't do it. I need him to know that Cait belongs to me. I need him to know that he can never have her again.

And now he does know.

"Glad to see you didn't jump over the bar and beat our bartender senseless."

I considered it. "Trust me. I wanted to."

"I could see that."

"You'd have done it too if it were you in my situation."

"Maybe."

"There's no maybe about it. When you love a woman the way I love Cait, there is no limit to what you'll do for her."

"Do you want to get out of here and go to another pub?"

"I've said what I needed to say and I'm good. It's over now. We can go somewhere else."

"Drinks are still on you, motherfucker."

"Fine."

32

CAITRIONA HUTCHESON

I ENTER OUR BEDROOM AND HUTCH IS SOUND ASLEEP. I can't believe he beat me home. I figured my girls' night out with Rachel would end long before his boys' night out with Brady.

Damn, he smells like whisky. I can smell it all the way across the room.

But I'm not mad. Hutch and Brady have been best mates for many years. I'm sure neither of them will admit it, but both of them must be sad they'll no longer see each other on a daily basis.

They won't be colleagues anymore. They won't live in the same town.

Hell, that makes me a little sad. And their final hoorah was well-deserved.

Hutch is Scottish. He holds his whisky well. And I usually enjoy our nights together after he's had a few drinks, but I'm not sure about tonight. He looks like he could be smashed.

"Hutch?" I shake his arm. "Hutch?"

He opens his eyes wide enough to form narrow

slits and smiles when he sees me. "Did you take the test yet?"

"No. I just got home from my girls' night out with Rachel. I'm taking it in the morning, remember?"

"Right."

He holds out his arm, lifting the covers. "Get into bed with me."

I climb into bed still wearing my clothes and nestle against my drunk husband.

"I love you, Lou."

"I love you too."

He pulls me close and kisses my forehead. "I met Cameron Stewart tonight."

I rise and prop on my elbows. "Whaaat?"

"He told me he wanted to shag you again, and I told him I would kill him if he ever touched you."

"Where the hell did you see Cameron? And how did that conversation even get started?"

"We'll talk about it tomorrow. It's late and I've had a lot to drink. Let's go to sleep."

It's only a minute or so before Hutch is drunk-snoring. Perfect. I get to listen to that all night.

I'm burning up so I get out of bed and take my clothes off. I'm completely naked when I crawl into bed next to my sleeping husband. He's naked too. For some reason, he strips down completely when he's had a lot to drink.

He rolls toward me, draping his bulky arm and heavy leg across my body. Not comfortable.

I lie beneath him wide awake as he continues to snore directly into my ear.

I'm not drunk but I wish I were because the alternative is that I'm horny. I want sex, but I'm guessing that'll probably be impossible since my husband is tanked.

I stare at the ceiling for a while and close my eyes. Just go to sleep. Go to sleep. Go to sleep.

Hutch stirs and his hand moves to cup my breast. It doesn't help matters at all.

I should probably feel ashamed for what I'm about to do, but I don't. Not even a little. Because what man would be angry about being awakened for sex?

"Hutch." He doesn't stir, so I shake his arm. "Hutch."

"Hmm." It's a groan, but not the sexy kind.

"I want you."

"What, mo maise?" His words are slightly slurred.

I wrap my hand around his cock, and damn, he's limp as a wet noodle. "Wake up."

While squeezing, I pump my hand up and down, and I can feel the blood beginning to fill his cock. "I want you to fuck me."

He jolts and his cock gets bigger and harder in my hand. "I'm up. I'm awake."

He attempts to sit up and then falls back against the bed. "I'm fucked up. You're going to have to get on top."

I move over and straddle him. He grips my hips and groans when I sink down his cock. "You feel so fucking good, mo maise."

He isn't wrong. It feels really good, but I already know I'm not going to come like this. I need more than penetration to get off, and Hutch is too incapacitated to do what it takes to get me there.

I'll have to do it for myself.

And I do.

Hutch barely comes before he passes out but it's okay. I got what I needed.

~

EVEN A HUNGOVER HUTCH STILL WAKES BEFORE ME. Amazing. I don't know how he does it.

I'm lying on my stomach and the bedsheet is draped over my bottom. His warm breath hits my skin, and then the slight scrape of his facial scruff moves along my lower back, followed by the kiss of his mouth. "It's morning, sleepyhead."

I lift my pillow and bury my head beneath it. "How are you so cheery this morning after a whisky drunk like last night?"

"I'm actually not cheery at all. I feel like shite, but I'm up because I'm dying for you to take the test." He crawls up my back and lies on top of me with his mouth at my ear. "Get your sweet bum into the loo and pee on that stick."

"Do you want to look at the results together?"

"Well, hell yes. You're not finding out before I do."

"Just making sure."

I scoot toward the edge of the bed and he catches my hand. "You know it's fine if it's not positive, right? That just means we'll get to keep trying, which isn't a bad alternative at all."

I nod. "I know."

I go into the bathroom and my bladder feels like it'll explode before I'm able to open the box and do the deed.

Your hopes were so high last month when you did this

test, and then it was negative. You were so disappointed. Let's not get too excited like you did last time, Cait. Everyone doesn't get pregnant on the first try. Or second. Sometimes it takes a little while. You know this. But also don't be afraid. You've made a baby with Hutch before. You can do it again. It'll happen.

I come out of the bathroom and sit beside him on the bed. He puts his arm around me and pulls me close, saying nothing. And that's okay. We don't have to say anything.

My phone chimes when the time is up, and I turn off the annoying sound.

"I love you no matter what."

"I know. Love you too."

Missionary? Unsuccessful.

The plow? Unsuccessful.

Reverse cowgirl? Definitely fun but successful? We're about to find out.

I inhale deeply as we walk into the bathroom and release the breath slowly as we stand over the test. It's amazing how the presence or absence of two lines inside the windows on this plastic stick has the power to dictate our happiness.

One bright pink line. And then a lighter-colored one next to it.

Two lines.

"This isn't what it looked like last month."

The directions said that a second line, even if light in color, was a positive as long as it was there. This is exactly what it looked like when I was pregnant the first time. "It looked different last month because it was negative."

"This is a positive result? You're pregnant?"

"Yes. I'm pregnant."

We reach for each other at the same time, squeezing tightly, and Hutch peppers kisses against the side of my face. "We did it, mo maise."

"Yes, we did." But I'm still mindful of what happened last time. "Let's not tell anyone yet."

"No one? Not even my parents?"

"I'd rather not until I reach twelve weeks. The chance of miscarriage becomes much lower after that point."

"That's a long time to wait when you're as excited as I am."

"Think of it this way. It can be a secret only the two of us get to share. That makes it special."

Hutch picks me up and carries me to the bed, depositing me on top like a fragile treasure. He lies beside me, his hand over my lower stomach. "How long will it be until you look pregnant?"

"I'm not really sure."

I've not been around a lot of pregnant women. Shannon was already pretty far along by the time I met her, and I avoided Heidi as much as possible.

I really know nothing about being pregnant. But I guess most women don't until it happens to them.

Hutch moves closer and presses the side of his face to my stomach. "Our wee bairn is inside you. Right there. That's amazing to me."

I push my fingers into his hair, stroking them over the scattered silver strands at his temples. "The whole thing is truly amazing when you think about it. This is our love story, our fairy tale, our destiny. This was fated from the moment your eyes met mine."

"We do have one hell of a love story, don't we?"

"Yes. A love story with a beautiful ever after."

EPILOGUE

CAITRIONA HUTCHESON

Go Hutch, go Hutch, go Hutch.

Don't let that bastard hook your stick again. And if he does, yank him off his fucking horse.

Hooking your opponent's stick is perfectly acceptable in polo. I've seen it done a million times, but I've never seen an opponent try to unseat Hutch from his horse the way this asshat is attempting to do so.

Hutch lifts his stick and strikes the ball, scoring another goal for his polo team, moving them into the winning position in the last minute of the final chukka.

Our two-year-old son is sitting on my lap and I grasp his hands, clapping them together, "Yay, James. Did you see Da? He scored another goal for the team. They're winning. Yaaay!"

Bonnie, our eight-year-old daughter, and Aleck, our five-year-old son, shoot out of their seats and celebrate their dad's goal. "Yaaay for Da."

Paden, our ten-year-old, is somewhere running

around with his friends, so I'm sure he missed this goal and the other ones too. That one is a busy little boy.

I look over to see if Ava Rose is cheering for her dad and find that she's gone from her usual spot where she and her friends sit. Where did she go? She was just there.

"Do you see where Ava Rose has gone?"

"I do," Clarissa says. I wait for her to tell me where she is, but she doesn't.

"Where?"

"I'm not sure you want to know."

I look over the rim of my sunglasses at Clarissa. "What are you talking about?"

"She and a young man are taking a walk together." Clarissa hesitates. "And holding hands while doing so."

Oh God.

Hutch will die.

And I may throw up and then die.

No, no, no. Not my baby. She's only twelve. She's too young for that.

"I hope Hutch doesn't see her with the boy, or he'll have a heart attack and fall off his horse." And then get trampled by that fool trying to unseat him.

"This is the natural order of things, Lou. You have to let go a wee bit."

It's only been a few weeks since Sara came home and caught Leo having sex with a girl in his bedroom. So, no, thank you. I'm not letting go.

"I can't tell Hutch." He will shit his white polo pants. And that will not be a good look on him.

"Ava Rose is growing up whether you tell him or not."

Uhh, shit. We have to go through this with four more kids? No, scratch that. *Five* more kids.

The game ends and Hutch's team wins. I'm thrilled about that. He's always in a good mood after a win.

I watch Hutch approaching and a thought occurs. My husband is forty-five years old and not a single one of these twenty-something-year-olds out here can fill out those pants like he does. Not a one of them is as sexy as he is.

To whomever decided polo players should wear fitted white pants... well played, madam. Well played. That in itself is a good enough reason to come watch men sit atop horses and hit a ball with a stick.

"Congratulations, sir. Great game."

"Thank you, mo maise." He leans forward and kisses my mouth. "There was a time or two I thought you might get to see me knocked on to my arse."

So I wasn't imagining it. "Who was that man trying to unseat you?"

"I believe that was Blair's most recent husband."

Really? She found a third fool to marry her? "Well, it looks like she married the right man this time. Because he's obviously..." I lower my voice. "...as big a bitch as she is."

Hutch shrugs. "Don't give a—" He looks at James, Aleck, and Bonnie. "We don't give a duck, do we?"

"Nope. No ducks given," Aleck says.

Oh God. One of these days they're going to figure out what duck really means.

"Are we ready to go, lads and lasses? Your da is tired and hungry."

Hutch usually eats an enormous meal and crashes after a game. But not tonight.

I lift my brows. "Clarissa and Gus are taking the kids home with them."

And I'm so grateful. I need this alone time with Hutch.

"Then I need hugs from my Hutcheson clan." He holds out his arms and is swarmed by ten little arms. "Is this a spend-the-night thing or are they coming home later?"

"Let them stay the night with us," Gus says.

Knowing the kids are out of the house and not within earshot would be so helpful. I'm not sure how Hutch is going to take this news.

He squats so he's on their level. Well, most of their levels. Ava Rose is already taller than I am. "Listen up, wee Hutcheson clan. You have to be good for Gussie and Nana."

Our five children sing, "Weee… willll."

"I love all of you and I'll see you tomorrow."

Five I-love-yous. It's so precious to hear coming from their sweet mouths.

And it'll soon be six.

Oh God. I may throw up.

The kids are taken care of. Now to move on to the scary, beautiful thing I must tell my husband. He's going to be a father again at forty-five. Maybe forty-six, depending on my due date.

He's going to… I don't know what he's going to do. But I have to make sure he takes off those white pants before I tell him.

～

MAXWELL HUTCHESON

WE SPEND EVERY MINUTE OF EVERY DAY BEING MUM and Da. And while I love it, I crave our special husband-and-wife alone time.

I get to have my wife to myself all night long without distractions or interruptions by the kids. I've been waiting for a moment like this for too long. We should send the kids to my parents' house more often.

We're barely through the front door when I pull Lou into my arms and kiss her. It begins slow and romantic but quickly escalates to heated and urgent. For once, the urgency isn't because we have to hurry and finish before we're interrupted by one of the kids.

"Tell me what you want, mo maise."

She touches my bottom lip with her finger. "I want to slow down. We're always in a rush and I'd like to take our time and enjoy each other."

I used to tease Lou by taking my time with her. I'd hold back and delay my orgasm for as long as possible. Sex went on and on. But that was before five kids.

"It's been a long time since we've taken things slowly."

We copulate on jackrabbit speed.

But not tonight.

She splays her hands on my chest and rubs my pecs. "I bought something new to wear for you."

Lou hasn't worn lingerie for me in a long time.

It's been far too long since I've seen her in something hot and sexy.

I grip the backs of her thighs and hike her up. She wraps her legs around my waist and I walk toward our bedroom. "You haven't carried me to bed in a long time."

"I'm going to be doing a lot of things tonight that I haven't done in a long time."

I lower her feet to the floor when we're in the bedroom and grip her bum. Pulling her against me, I move my mouth over her ear. "Go put on the lingerie. And don't keep me waiting too long. I'm ready to be inside you."

"Will you light the candles while I change?"

"I will do anything you tell me to."

She grabs my face and pulls me in for a quick kiss. "I won't be long."

The candles give the room the perfect romantic ambience. It's a good reminder for taking things slowly.

I'm undressing when Lou comes out of the bathroom. She's wearing a pink lace slip and she looks hot as hell in it. Her tits look fantastic, even after nursing four of our kids. She's wearing a mischievous grin, and I know why when she turns around and shimmies, showing me the ruffles over her bum. "Like it?"

My cock immediately swells inside of my Y-fronts. "You look so fucking hot, babe. Come here."

The way she walks toward me is beguiling. Each step she takes seduces my mind and body. I must remind myself of what I'm to do—take my time and enjoy Lou. My wife. My lover. My NOLA girl and partner in life. The mother of my children.

I place one hand at her lower back and cradle her face with my other. She covers my hand with her own and closes her eyes, appearing as though she's completely savoring the feel of my skin against hers. "Twelve years later and the simple touch of your hand still feels like pure seduction."

"All you have to do is breathe and I want to be inside you."

We move to the bed and she lies down on the middle. I begin at her ankles, kissing my way up her body, which still looks amazing after four babies. She occasionally complains about stretch marks and her stomach being fleshy instead of flat, but I don't see flaws when I look at her. She's perfect to me.

Pushing up her slip, I look at the tiny scrap of knickers covering her in the front. I push my fingers under the elastic waistband and tug. She lifts her bum and I drag the pink lace down her legs.

After tossing her knickers on the floor, I migrate up her body slowly. When we're face-to-face, I cradle her cheeks with both of my hands. "I love you, mo maise."

"And I love you, my hot Scot."

She brings her legs up around my waist and wiggles beneath me until I'm positioned at her drenched opening. "I was planning to go down on you."

She shakes her head. "Later. Right now, I want you inside me."

She squeezes her legs to coax me closer and I glide in slowly. I push her legs back, bending them out and she tilts her hips. I thrust in and out several times, and she meets each one, bringing me deeper inside her.

"I miss this, Lou. Being so deep we become one with no beginning and no end."

I move my hand to where we're joined and briefly enjoy feeling myself sliding in and out of her before I seek out her clit. We may be making love instead of fucking hard, but I'm still making sure my girl comes.

She moans when I find the spot and I circle it with my fingers. "Does that feel good?"

"Oh yeah," she moans. "Right there. Don't stop."

She tenses and squeezes her legs tightly, signaling the onset of her climax, and then I feel the magnificent way her body squeezes my cock. That, combined with the knowledge of knowing I've brought her to orgasm, ignites the onset of my undoing. I thrust a few more times and then drive deep inside her, emptying all of myself.

Still blanketing her with my body, I kiss her forehead and lift my head so I can see her face. "Hi."

She smiles and giggles. "Hi."

She releases her legs from around my waist, but I'm not ready to pull out. This is a rare occasion these days. I want to stay like this for just a little bit longer.

I lower my face to hers and gently scrape her with my facial hair. "I love the way your beard feels against my face."

"I've been thinking of shaving it."

"No! Absolutely not. It's sexy as hell and I love the way it feels against my skin."

"Okay, okay. I'll keep it if it makes you happy."

I plant a quick kiss against her mouth before pulling out and rolling to my back. I reach to take her hand in mine, lacing our fingers. I still have to be touching her in some way after sex.

We lie motionless and I savor the post-sex bliss and luxury of being sprawled naked. And a thought occurs to me: I'm actually going to get to fuck my wife a second time tonight. That never happens anymore.

"What do you want for your birthday?"

Well, that was out of the clear blue.

"I don't know." Why is she asking about my birthday? It's so far away.

"I have a gift for you. But I don't know how you're going to feel about it."

"I always love your gifts. You know that."

"You didn't ask for this gift."

"Sometimes those are the best kinds of gifts."

Lou takes my hand and puts it on her stomach. She places her hand on top of mine and presses down. "Your gift is right here."

I rise from the bed so I can see her face. "Are you... pregnant?"

She nods and tears fill her eyes. "I am."

I look at our hands on top of her stomach. "How far along?"

"I'm not sure yet. Maybe six weeks."

Another baby.

"Are you feeling unwell?" With each pregnancy, Lou has been sick through the fourth month.

"I've been fine so far."

Another baby.

"How long have you known?"

"Two days."

Another baby.

"Did you wait to tell me because you were afraid of my reaction?"

"Maybe."

I rub my hand over her stomach in a circular motion, same as I did the other times she was pregnant, and it still amazes me. "It's right there beneath my hand. Already forming and growing."

I place my head on her stomach. "I want this baby. I already love him or her. Don't worry for one second that I don't. You and our children are my heart and now this baby is too."

"Just as you are mine. Always."

The End

ABOUT THE AUTHOR

Georgia Cates is the New York Times, USA Today, and Wall Street Journal Best-Selling Author. She resides in rural Mississippi with her wonderful husband, Jeff, and their two beautiful daughters. She spent fourteen years as a labor and delivery nurse before she decided to pursue her dream of becoming an author and hasn't looked back yet.

Sign-up for Georgia's newsletter at
www.georgiacates.com.
Get the latest news, first look at teasers,
and giveaways just for subscribers.

Stay connected with Georgia at:
Twitter, Facebook, Tumblr, Instagram,
Goodreads and Pinterest.

Made in the USA
San Bernardino, CA
30 June 2019